FALLEN SAINTS

FALLEN SAINTS

PAUL V. CWIAKALA

Silk Baron Independent Press
Paterson, New Jersey

Published in the United States by Silk Baron Independent Press.
First Edition: December 2014

Cover Illustration Copyright © 2012 by Wenart Gunadi
Cover design by Silk Baron Independent Press
Book design and production by Silk Baron Independent Press
Editing by Silk Baron Independent Press

Silk Baron Independent Press
www.silkbaronindependentpress.com

To my family and friends, thank you for putting up with my years of ranting and rambling.

Table of Contents

Chapter One

Fireballs whizzed by as Angie dove into the dust behind the outhouse on the north end of the run down ranch, a cloud of it puffing up as she plopped - she breathed it in in quick ragged breaths. No time to cough: she snapped open her Colt Paterson and began reloading. Another fireball smacked the top of the outhouse, the flimsy wood splintering into charred shards. As each bullet slid into place, Angie could picture each damnable fool responsible for putting her in this dire predicament.

First, as always, there was that fat mustachioed bastard Wilson. She could see him now, sitting all-so-comfortable in his tacky office back in Verdopolis, sipping his midafternoon brandy and eyeing the safe where he kept the stack of Treasury notes promised upon apprehension. Him and his beady blue eyes, his half-moon of thinned blonde hair, that stupid half-smile whenever he'd claim to have "just the right job", the slick of sweat on that fat nose and those fat cheeks.

Angie swore to herself: this time she would plant her fist in his face.

Another bullet followed by another plume of flame, dirt, and burnt shrubbery. Let's not forget the villain of the day, of course: a particularly nasty miracle worker of the so-called "Order" His name escaped her. Not that the name was particularly important, it never was. They'd tracked him to some abandoned ranch somewhere south of Moab, pretty country really, something she was sure some artist from back east could really appreciate with all the canyons and vast open land and beige-brown-reddish stone all around. They'd barely tied up the horses when the conflagration got underway.

Which brought Angie to the man she rode all the way out here with.

"You still alive out there, Mr. Carnation?" she shouted. The whisper of desert wind and the crackle of embers answered. Angie snapped her Colt Paterson shut. "Andrew?"

She growled, wiped a sweaty lock of hair from her forehead and dared to peek around the corner. Nothing. Nothing, but for the dilapidated and crumbling side of the ranch house and the bare (or burning) land as far as she could see. A shadow moved in the window, Angie shot at it and ran before a blast obliterated the outhouse. She slammed into the back of the ranch house, half by her own momentum and half the force of the explosion. The entire house rattled, threatening to come down on the bastard's head (if only there was a ceiling left to collapse). She cocked the Paterson again and, with a woman's tenderness, slid along the house's back wall toward a gaping maw that had once been a window but now served as a rear entrance. Her ears twitched with each creak of wood she created, and doubly so for those she did not.

Angie reached the hole and paused for a breath, to well up her grit…and then the entire side of the house was reduced to timbers, pulled apart by forces well beyond her comprehension. All she could do was react, to turn and fire once, twice, at the dark-hooded figure that stood in the wall's place. Either she missed in her panic or he deflected them with some sort of magic, flicked aside as a child flicks marbles, but she knew as she stumbled backward and the remains of the wall rained around her that neither bullet had struck. A yellow-toothed smile was all she could make out from under the hood, the only movement from the otherwise stone-still robes.

"You should never have come after me," he said. A flick of the wrist, and Angie was flung through the air like a puppet connected to its master by piano wire. She slammed into an ancient cupboard in what had once been the pantry, the wood disintegrating into chips as she landed hard beside an old fireplace. Angie coughed out dust, her bowler rolling out of arm's reach and her hair askew in all directions. The miracle worker tilted his head, his smile unchanged and otherwise unmoving, she never saw him turn to face her.

"A woman," he said, in a tone that could be mistaken for delight. "Fascinating."

As suddenly as she could muster, Angie rolled and took aim for the bastard's chest. Somehow he was able to predict this and, with the same miraculous power that had tossed her across the room, flung her gun away and pulled her throat to his palm.

He began to squeeze.

Angie flailed, her nails digging into the miracle worker's hand but unable to get between his fingers and her tightened throat. She kicked him, but if he felt it he didn't show any sign. The bastard wouldn't even look her in the eye, but just kept smiling that god damned grin.

"Why did you get yourself involved?" he said. "This had nothing to do with you. My business is with the Brotherhood, not you."

He must've felt her attempting to spit out a flurry of unladylike curses, so he loosened his grip - ever so slightly - for Angie to growl:

"I just want the damn reward…"

"Foolish harlot," the miracle worker said. "You need more than mere bullets to match with the holy powers at my disposal. Even an altar boy knows this." That grin somehow widened. "Now, die."

The hand squeezed again, Angie could feel her veins pulsing, desperate to pump the blood through. Her lungs craved sweet air. She kicked at the miracle worker more ferociously than before, stabbing her spurs into his sides and his legs, but to no avail. Amidst all this, she spotted her gun on the floor, resting in what would've been the corner of the room. Panicked thoughts of one weapon drew her to memories of another and she reached for her second gun: a .38 caliber revolver hidden under her coat in the small of her back, an emergency weapon she swore would only be used for -

CRUNCH!

Suddenly, she was free. Angie breathed in too big a gulp of air and coughed several times. As she found her breath, she realized that the miracle worker was down as well, and screaming: flailing just as she was only moments before. Only, rather than cold strangulation, he'd been pounced upon by a hulking amalgamation of man and coyote, its eyes amber-red and its jaws clamped down on the miracle worker's shoulder. The pair struggled, the man -coyote shaking the miracle worker with all its might, and the man pathetically slamming the creature's head with his free elbow. Blood gushed from the wound, soaking the miracle worker's robe and the creature's desert-colored fur, splattering across the dust-soaked floorboards.

At last, Angie came to her senses and drew her revolver. She aimed for the creature.

"Let him go!"

It eyed her, slowing but not stopping the maiming.

"Do it! Now!"

A long time ago, though perhaps not as long as she'd convinced herself, Angie had developed the habit of counting after such threats.

One...two...

She'd never decided what number was the limit, and cursed herself each time for it.

...Seven...eight...

Her stomach turned cold. Not like this. Not here. Not over a lowlife murderer not worth the money on his head.

...Eleven...twelve...

Regaining his senses, the miracle worker attempted to perform another incantation, but was too slow: with a single powerful swing, the man-coyote threw the miracle worker through the last remaining wall. He landed with a thud and a pained cry about twenty yards away. With the revolver still trained on the creature, Angie sprinted for the edge of the house and scooped up her Colt Paterson, aiming that at the downed miracle worker.

Well, the once-downed miracle worker. Despite a chunk of flesh and bone torn from him, he hadn't passed out: instead, the fool was trying to run. The man-coyote turned from Angie to his intended prey, ignoring the gun aimed square at skull.

"Goddamn fool," Angie muttered, and then shouted after the miracle worker: "Stop!"

He ignored her. She fired. He fell, just short of the broken-down fence that surrounded this ruin.

The distraction ended, Angie aimed both pistols at the man-coyote. It did not look at her, nor advance in any threatening way - in fact, it cowered, almost like a puppy would knowing its master was angry. And boy was she angry.

"Andrew," she said. "What have I told you about turning?"

It made a whimpering noise. She lowered the guns slightly, but did not take her eyes off of him.

"Are you in control?"

It nodded. A single crimson droplet rolled off its snout and made a new tiny puddle on the floor.

"Are you sure?"

It nodded again. She let herself exhale and her arms swing to her sides.

"You're a damn fool, you know that?" Angie said, holstering her weapons.

"Especially this close to the full moon. I could've killed you, was this close to doing it this time, too." She bent over to pick up her bowler. "And for goodness' sake, cover yourself. You're human being, not a wild animal. Although sometimes, I do wonder."

Chapter Two

New Mexico, October 1909

Verdopolis was splayed out in a shape that reminded Angie of a flattened lemon, bisected by the railroad that wound in from the mountains east toward the Pacific far to the west. The nicest portion was south of the tracks – that was where the silver barons and the local heavy-duties lived, with all the niceties that went along with that. North of the tracks, where the common folk generally lived, was seedier: the north side was filled with saloons, and industry, and the leeches of society.

Situated in the desert at the edge of the so-called civilized world, the town persisted as one of the few "wild" places left out on the former frontier. It had started as little more than pit stop for wagon trains on their way to the west coast, upgrading to a stop for locomotives when the railroad came through forty years ago. It probably would've remained that way had a vein of silver not been found in the nearby foothills - it wasn't long before the place thrived with prospectors, entrepreneurs, and villainy.

Despite the railroad, this end of New Mexico territory was remote and in practice beyond the reach of Federal law: Verdopolis and the other towns in this region were effectively independent city-states, run by ruthless men who cared little for the residents and much for their own fortunes. Though not born in Verdopolis, Angie had come to consider it as close to a home as she'd ever had since childhood.

For the last three years, the region was embroiled in a bloody feud between two warring factions of clerics, or miracle workers as they were often called: the Brotherhood and the Order.

The Brotherhood was mysterious to Angie, their origins shrouded in mystery, although less literally and more due to a personal apathy. Brotherhood miracle workers were religious fanatics from back east, where they'd suffered discrimination and had been considered outcasts for their rather radical beliefs - anti-industrial, anti-capitalist, anti-intellectual. Although their spiritual leader remained there, many of the group's followers had fled out to the territories over the last ten years. They saw themselves as modern Merry Men to their leader's Robin Hood, opposing the wealthy and powerful in favor of the poor and hungry. Somewhat admirable, although she was not fond for their penchant for violence against those they disapproved of. She'd even heard rumors that the lawmen were investigating on suspicions of seditious plots against the government.

Their rivals, the Order, were easier to understand but no less repugnant. The Order arose shortly after the Brotherhood arrived in the territory, about a decade ago, amongst the miracle workers already established from the mainline denominations as a specific counterpoint to the Brotherhood. Wherever the Brotherhood would go, you could be sure to find the Order not far behind.

Until the bloodshed started, most in the territory supported the Order, but now most were disgusted with the group's vigilantism and murder in the name of God and Justice, or their own skewed vision of those at least. Lawmen from the Sheriff on up to the Governor have tried to arbitrate or mediate, but thus far little success had been made. Good thing, too, 'cause Angie wasn't sure what she'd do if the bounties dried up.

Wilson sat up as Angie threw the door open, anticlimactically heralded by the little ding-ding of the bell meant to announce the arrival of less angry visitors.

"Mrs. Grissom?" he said. Wilson fiddled with the ledger he was doodling in a moment before she arrived.

"You haven't caught our dear Order friend so soon, have you?" Angie quelled the urge to shoot him, instead slowly taking off her bowler and running her slender fingers through her hair. Wilson's office changed little between her visits: his desk was neat, with papers arranged in nice even stacks and not a single thing seeming out of place. Behind the desk there was a set of shelves, each filled with stacks of books and papers, some business related and some not, though she'd never paid close enough attention to know any real detail about what Wilson kept on it. The office had many windows, wrapping around along the wall behind her and along the wall to her left, outside which she could make out the corner of Main Street and what had come to be known as Connor's Way, after a certain hooligan by that name was found stabbed to death outside the saloon a few doors down years back.

Wilson was in his mid-forties, and though it didn't look it was indeed married - had been for twenty years - though Angie had never once heard him mention his wife by name. She knew he'd been born and raised in Ohio by his accent, and gathered from talk around town that he'd arrived with the rush of silver prospectors when the mines were discovered, though had given up on that rather quickly before settling into bail bonds. A close friend of the local Judge, Wilson was among the first to get wind of any new bounties issued by the court in Verdopolis. Angie knew Wilson through a mutual friend of her late husband, so when she began hunting bounties they were introduced and an arrangement was struck: whatever Wilson heard first from his Judge friend, Angie would hear first from Wilson. It had paid off handsomely several times, but Wilson, being a coward and not the fighting sort, would often have no clue what hunting a fugitive actually entailed and thus had grossly inaccurate expectations for how "easy" or "difficult" a job would be. Angie knew he had some measure of education, although she doubted it was formal and most of his business sense probably came from his father, who was rumored to run a general store in Cincinnati.

"No, Wilson, things did not go quite as planned," she said. Her eyes narrowed. "Nor as smooth as you implied."

The flabby moron appeared clueless, like a dumb animal completely oblivious to the rifle aimed at its brow.

"Oh?"

"Oh, indeed," Angie said. She took a seat in a chair opposite Wilson's desk. "Wilson, there are two kinds of miracle workers in this world: the majors and the minors. Now, a minor miracle worker I have no particular problem tracking down so long as the courts are willing to pay up. Those minors, they ain't no more trouble than the typical lay man. But the majors? A major can hit harder and run farther than a normal man, can cure himself of most anything that ain't fatal, and atop all that can toss people about like ragdolls without even laying a finger or throw balls of holy fire if they so choose. Majors, they're serious goddamn trouble."

"I take it Brother Mills was not a minor miracle worker," Wilson said.

"No, he was not," Angie said.

"Were you able to apprehend him?"

"He's dead."

"That's a damn shame," Wilson said. He shook his head and began fiddling with his ledger again, attempting to pretend he had not just realized the sedate fury he was confronted with. Wilson had never been a brave man, even as a boy he cowered in fear from danger - it's a wonder he'd ever found his way this far from comfortable Cincinnati. "He's no good to me dead, my dear. Certainly not worth twenty five dollars, that is for sure. Not for a corpse."

Angie rapped her nails on the Colt Paterson's handle.

"He wasn't worth twenty five dollars alive, either. He was worth at least twice as much for all the trouble he gave us," she said. Wilson gulped. Angie smiled and leaned forward just a little, resting an elbow on Wilson's desk. He leaned back in his seat and loosened his collar with a single pudgy finger.

"Listen, Mrs. Grissom, I'm sure you can understand the predicament I am in," Wilson said. "I doubt the courts will honor our arrangement if I cannot deliver their fugitive so he can undergo due process of the law, and if my arrangement is not honored then our arrangement is, by right and proper extension, dishonored as well."

"So, you're not going to pay me?" Angie said. Wilson shook his head, his puffy cheeks swaying slower and longer than the rest, and waved his hands in an exaggerated denial.

"No, no, no! I didn't say that," he said. "I'd like to propose another bounty..."

"Excuse me?" Angie said, at last letting her anger shine through. "I come in here expecting the twenty five dollar reward I was promised by you and the Sheriff, and you want me to go back out there again? You're out of your damn fool mind if you think I'm walking out of here without what I'm rightly owed!"

"I told you, I cannot in good faith pay you for the miracle worker..."

Angie bolted to her feet, a hand clearly resting on her

Colt Paterson. It would take only the flick of her wrist and…

"However, I trust you, Mrs. Grissom." Wilson had gone sweaty and pale, he stumbled over his words. "I…I know you're good to your word, and … um … if you say the miracle worker's posted bounty was unfairly low - although, I do have some personal doubts on the matter - then, I'll concede it must have been too low. So, it is only fair and proper that I'll pay you double what you're owed, plus the reward for the very simple job I would like to offer you."

"…How simple?"

Wilson stood, waddled to the desk on the shelf behind him, and leafed through a stack of wanted posters and bounty postings. He finally found what he was looking for and handed it to Angie.

"The fugitive's name is 'Sell-eron'." The posting read 'Celeron Sambucci'. "Bounty's thirty five dollars, alive." Angie examined the sketch: the man looked young, younger than Andrew even, and was handsome, with sharply cut hair and somber oval eyes. He wore eyeglasses, and based on what little dress the posting showed did not appear to be a miracle worker. The impression was of someone far too well-to-do to be on any wanted poster.

"What did he do?" she said.

"He's a thief, I believe," Wilson said, huffing as he sat again. "Not really a career criminal, I'm told, more of a professorial type from back east. According to my dear friend Judge Breckenridge, this Mr. Sambucci had until very recently been a guest of the monks at the Monastery of the Knights of Saint James the Just. You know, that rather modest place up in the Sangre de Cristo Mountains?

Not exactly sure what the fellow was doing there, but when he left he took with him a certain book that seems to be of particular value to the holy men there."

"How valuable?" Angie said. Wilson laughed.

"Evidently it is their holy of holies," he said. "An old copy of the Bible, very old. They seem to think it's one of the very first ones, written by Saint Peter, given to Christ's brother Saint James, and passed down from the Apostles through the ages to them. You would think their order would at the very least keep such a thing under lock and key if it were truly so valuable."

She folded up the posting and stuffed it in her long coat's pocket.

"I'll take ten dollars up front, and you'll have yourself a deal."

"But, I said…"

"I know what you said."

Wilson closed his eyes, seemed to attempt mustering some courage to repel her, but upon failing just sighed and opened his desk drawer.

+ + +

The Alamos Garage sat just beyond town, on the road that ran west alongside the railroad. It was once a farm or ranch years and years back, though hadn't been for as long as Angie could remember: there was the old house, with the creaky porch, peeling paint, and one cracked window to the left of the front door. Around the side was the old barn, converted into a carriage house for the professional tinkerer who lived here. It had been a while since she peered in there, but she could easily remember the workbench covered in its various hammers, forceps, and other tools; the place, with its high ceiling and rows of broken down or not quite yet repaired carriages, always had the air of a wizard's workshop – a sense that held her even beyond childhood into her early womanhood. And while the place didn't look so much different now as she stepped through those ten foot tall doors again, one thing had changed: along with the traditional horse drawn carts, carriages, and stagecoaches she remembered there were also a couple of new "motorcars", those new horseless carriages she'd seen once or twice in her travels.

Although she'd seen motorcars before, such high technology wasn't exactly easy to come across in the territory, not unless one had a fortune or a contact. In Angie's case, her contact was Mr. Alamos, who at the moment was buried underneath a particularly beat up tangle of green metal parked in what would've been a horse's stall, muttering curses between clangs of metal against metal. For a moment, she wondered how the motorcar had found itself in such a sorry state. She tipped back her bowler and leaned against a post.

"Old man, you under there?" she said. Her uncle crawled out from under the car, his face, hands, and shirt black with dirt. Joshua Alamos was older, his hair sharp silver tinged with charcoal black and face ragged with the deep creases of age, work, and worry. Despite that, he was still tall and strongly-built – well-enough in shape to take on any man half his age. His chocolate eyes showed no sign of senility, and he spoke with the careful precision of a master linguist. He was part native, Choctaw, although Angie only knew that because of their history. She kept quiet on the suspicion that he didn't want many to know. Uncle Joshua's smile was bright, as if her visit had been the sole beam of light in what had otherwise been a dismal day.

"Angie!" he said. "Now, here's a sight I didn't expect. It's been far too long!" The big man embraced her, smearing her face with soot. Angie allowed herself to return the embrace.

"It's good to see you too," Angie said.

"Where's that young friend of yours? Andrew, wasn't it?"

"Busy entertaining himself."

Joshua invited her into the house and, after cleaning himself up, offered food and drink. Angie turned down the food, but accepted the whiskey. As always, Joshua wanted to reminisce and talk about the "good old times", back before she got into bounty hunting, when she was just a little girl sent to live with her aunt and uncle, or even earlier when he was a boy living on the frontier. He was born and raised in New Mexico, the third son of bean farmers, but went east during the war to look for better work. He wouldn't talk about it, but she suspected he fought for the Confederates in Arkansas – an old limp and a plethora of scars suggested a tale of utmost heroism and brutality. Sometimes, late at night, he'd mumble in his sleep about someone named "the Colonel", "the wall", and a few other phrases nonsensical without context.

After the war, Joshua headed back west along with the silver rush to Verdopolis. There, he met his wife, Susanna, and gave up mining to start tinkering with carriages and engines so they could start a family. When motorcars came along years later, Joshua would be about the only man in Verdopolis at all qualified to repair the contraptions. Joshua had a son who he hadn't seen or heard from in years, and whom Angie had never met. When younger, she thought he was dead, but every couple years a letter would come from some far off corner of the map sending greetings and assurances. Susanna, as it happens, was Angie's maternal aunt. After her mother passed, Angie was sent to live with Susanna and Joshua. They were good to her and Joshua treated her as if she were his own, even after Susanna passed to consumption in the Spring of '91.

But the memories, besides being painful, were only distractions. There was work to be done.

"So, you've got yourself a couple of motorcars?" Angie said. Angie, sitting at the table, watched Joshua try to start a fire in the hearth. Watching the back of his head, she imagined him smiling as she said that.

"Yep," he said. "The Quadricycle is a wreck, been at that for a week now and haven't been able to get the motor running. The other one, the Model N, is in perfect condition; just had a bent crank is all. It belongs to Anderson Mitchell, the banker over in Azulopolis. You know, the one who was caught sleeping with the reverend's wife a few years back? Said he'd be back for it three weeks ago, but hasn't shown yet. Startin' to hope he never comes back, though – that thing is a beaut! Best damn thing to come out of the Motor Company yet, in my oh-so-humble opinion."

The flames seemed to catch at last and Joshua moved back a bit. Angie swirled her whiskey.

"Do you suppose I could borrow the Model N?"

Joshua stood. Above the hearth hung a framed photograph of Joshua and Aunt Susanna, the only photo taken of her before she passed. He began fiddling with the frame, trying to straighten what was already in perfect order.

"Where are you headed?"

"Rio del Cobardes," Angie said. "That small place near the border. You remember it?"

"I remember the town. The Southern Pacific rides through there, doesn't it? You don't need a motorcar," he said.

"Not for a few years now, they haven't."

"Still, you don't need a motorcar to get there. Care to tell me what's so important that you need to get there so fast?" he said. Angie sipped her whiskey. Her stomach fluttered.

"Work. Just work," she said. He turned to face her, half his body silhouetted by the fire and the smile wiped from his face by a look she was all too familiar with, disappointment. She tried to stare him down, to fight past it, but after a moment Angie just averted her eyes. She maintained her poker face, but inside winced at what was coming. She always winced, but made a point of never letting anyone know it.

"You know you can do better than this," Joshua said. "You're better than bounty hunting and gunslinging. You're a lady, an attractive one at that, and you've still got your youth. Why are you throwing it all away with this nonsense? You were grieving when this all started, I understand that, but that was almost ten years ago now. Angela, you have to move on."

"I'm not doing this for my personal entertainment," she said. The words came out in a near-hiss. "We've got bills to pay. Have you already forgotten how much money you owe that bastard rancher Charlie Ingham? Nearly two thousand dollars still, I reckon. Where do you suppose we're going to get the money to pay that?"

"I can manage," Joshua said. Now it was his turn to avoid eye contact.

"Like hell you can," Angie said. "Only reason Mr. Ingham hasn't seized everything we have as collateral is the money I bring in with my un-feminine exploits! Unless you got some extra money lying around in secret, I don't think you're going to make fifty dollars by the end of the month. This job I'm on, I'm gonna be paid almost twice that. You're getting old, Uncle Josh. One of these days, you're liable to get hurt or sick or just plain too damn old. Then, where will we be?"

"It's not just about the money for you," he said, approaching the table. "You may be able to fool that poor Cajun boy, but you can't fool me. You think putting down that gun means you're letting Elijah go."

He stood over her, still as big and imposing a man as he was when Angie was only a girl.

"And you'd be right."

Angie finished her drink, letting the burn in her throat distract her from how deeply Joshua's words cut, and stood.

"Can I have the motorcar or not?"

Joshua tried to beg through his eyes, but she would have none of it. He sighed, shaking his head ever so slightly as he did, and walked past her into the bedroom.

"Of course you can."

Angie straightened her bowler. Her heart was beating fast, she took a breath and tried to calm herself again.

"Thanks for the whiskey and the motorcar," she said. Joshua didn't answer.

+ + +

It was along a destitute side street called Orient Way, its shadows lit by red oil lanterns in those dark spaces where the red light of sunset couldn't penetrate, where Angie found ramshackle tenement known colloquially around town as "Bertha's". It wasn't the first time she'd ascended these crumbling steps, or coldly pushed past the technicolored harlot puffing away on the stoop, or gagged at the stench of sweat, filth, cigars, opium, and cheap perfume when she entered the front hall. A second woman, her graying hair bunched up like a wild pineapple and dressed in barely concealing red robes with frayed black lacing, sat at the foot of an interior staircase as decrepit as those out front. She smirked at the sight at Angie, wisps of cigarette smoke escaping in lazy thin waves from her smeared ruby lips.

"He's upstairs," she said, stabbing and twisting the half -burnt tobacco tube into the wall. "Second door on the right." Angie didn't acknowledge the harlot at all, but as she stepped past her on the stairs the woman shook her head and, that smirk still certainly plastered on, whispered something under her breath. Angie could've taken a moment to parse it out, but decided to grit her teeth instead. She wasn't interested in having it out with a back-alley whore.

Besides, it took only a moment to find her quarry: in the candle-lit decrepit hall, tongue-deep in a girl she'd come to assume was a favorite, arms enveloped around each other like vines hugging an old post. At least Andrew was mostly dressed this time.

Andrew Carnation was a skinny kid, just shy of twenty -five years old, and not bad to look at - downright handsome, in fact: fair-skinned, fair-haired, sky blue eyes, soft rounded cheeks, and an impeccable smile. This, along with his naturally good temper, conspired to make him easily sociable. It was not hard for Mr. Carnation to make friends, even amongst the sordid lot they tended to associate with, and even less difficult to make his way into the brassiere of any lady.

Except Angie herself, that is. She never quite saw what everyone else did in the boy, though perhaps that had to do more with the circumstances of their meeting than any deep immunity to his charms. Had it really only been a bit more than three years since she'd first heard his name muttered through Winston's lips, just another wanted outlaw to hunt? A runaway from Louisiana, he was wanted in connection to some bloody business out in East Texas. Winston had made it seem he was deadly dangerous, a real hard bruiser. What Angie had found...

Andrew's slut spotted Angie first, her eyes immediately drifting to the Colt Paterson, and yelped, pulling Andrew close - and between them.

"Huh?" Andrew glanced over his shoulder. "Oh, hey. I was just leaving."

"Is that your wife?" The slut said, still cowering behind him. Andrew laughed, so hearty that he took a step back and eyes squeezed shut. Angie just blinked, and fought her hand's urge to inch toward her pistol.

"What? No, no," he said. "She's my partner. Business partner."

"Oh." She didn't sound convinced. Andrew just kept smiling, and gently gripped her petite chin between his thumb and forefinger.

"Don't you worry your fine little self. I'll be seeing you around, I'm sure."

Andrew turned back toward Angie, his expression little changed, and motioned back toward the stairs. Not another word was spoken until the pair had cleared Orient Way into a less distasteful part of town.

"Thank you."

"For what?" Andrew said. Angie eyed him, crooking her lips into the smallest of smiles.

"Not making me wait again."

"Oh!" He half-coughed, half-laughed the word. "I don't quite plan on giving you the opportunity to kick in the door and shove your pistols into another poor girl's face. Somewhat difficult to get them into the mood to finish again!"

Angie punched him in the arm. Perhaps it would be more accurate to say she was immune to only some of his charm.

"And how did your business go? Did you get the money?"

he said.

"Not quite," Angie said. Andrew stepped in front, his smile fading fast.

"Not quite? What does that mean?"

"It means Winston is a lowlife fool," she said. She paused as a pair of pedestrians passed them, big men in pinstripe vests and neatly cut beards, carrying on a conversation of their own. She resumed with stern resolve. "And that we have a new job."

Andrew rolled his eyes and let her pass, following inevitably as a puppy follows its master.

"Is it as suicidal as the last?" he said.

"Not quite."

"There's that 'not quite' again…"

Angie turned, grabbed hold of Andrew's collar, and pulled him close, hissing:

"The only thing making this job at all suicidal is you!"

She released him and resumed walking, leaving Andrew somewhat bewildered as he stumbled after her.

"What does that mean?"

"It means that you may be a decent shot with a rifle, Mr. Carnation, but you are a difficult man to rely on," she said. "You are not fond of following my directions, although I have been doing this for nearly twice as long as you have…

"Well, hold on one moment there…"

"…You have a tendency to get yourself into bigger trouble than you can manage…"

"Wait, Angie, if you'd just…"

"…And the full moon is in four days."

Andrew stopped following. After a few more steps, Angie paused herself and turned back: Andrew's eyes glistened with frustration.

"I haven't forgotten," he said.

When Angie finally met Andrew - the real Andrew, not the monster he became once a month - he was a frightened boy, confused and horrified. He'd been cursed out in the Louisianan bayou and fled to Texas, fearing what he'd do when the full moon came. What he did was slaughter twelve men at a brothel outside Palestine, one of them a Sheriff's deputy. She eventually caught up with him months after that, and it was her choice to either shoot him dead or take him along. That was the day she started the counting habit.

"I know you haven't," Angie said. "Your visits to Orient Way are like clockwork. I know why you go, and it's not the attitude I need from my business partner before starting a job."

"I can't help…" He cut himself off as a pair of older ladies, dolled-up in fine lavender dresses and one twirling a parasol, strolled by. Andrew forced a courteous smile and tipped his hat. "…Help what I've become. This is what I have to live with, not you, and this is how I deal with it."

Angie stepped closer, her voice hushed:

"And you know how I deal with it."

He averted his eyes and, slowly, nodded.

"I almost did it last time."

"I know. I'm sorry."

"Can you control yourself this time?" Angie said. "'Cause if not, I'll be more than happy to leave you behind,

Mr. Carnation."

"I can control it," he said. The smile and the charm returned. "Don't you worry about me. This coyote's staying locked in his cage."

Angie smiled.

"Good."

The two began their stroll again.

"So, what's the job?

Chapter Three

Rio del Cobardes sat on the fringe of the American ex-frontier and the Mexican desert wilderness.

It had started as a trading post set up by frontiersmen on the banks of the dried-up brook that lent its name, dealing in furs and trinkets from the local tribes and Spanish missionaries in exchange for just as useless junk from the East. Much like Angie's home, the place went through a boom when a copper vein was found in the nearby foothills - big enough to warrant an extension of the railroad.

It wasn't long before it dried up and Rio del Cobardes shriveled. The miners and the railroad left, leaving the traders, missionaries, and those aboriginals who hadn't been slaughtered or shipped to the Indian Territory left with a town more dead than alive.

Perhaps it was that stillness that unnerved Angie as she drove the autocar down what had been the main avenue. Boards were missing from one building. What had been the doctor's office had its windows broken, the glass that remained jagged and dusted just like an ancient mountain range, a shutter hung from only one hinge swinging to and fro in a lazy, erratic, endless swing. Everything was dry or dried out, broken down or blackened with dust. If she didn't know better already, she might have thought Rio del Cobardes' had shuddered its last since her last visit.

"Huh. Nice place," Andrew said.

Angie eased the motorcar to a stop in front of the saloon: a wide squat mudbrick building, its windows laced with fractures and an awning that didn't seem to have seen the working end of a hammer or felt the prick of nails in maybe a generation or so. Yet, this place was the first to yield any sign of life: voices, the clinks of glass and metal, the shuffle of feet and chairs. Several patrons raised their heads as the bounty hunters walked through the doorless hole that served as an entrance. Her eyes darted amongst the hard eyes and salted beards, fighting her hand's itch to reach for the Colt Paterson, but she recognized no one of importance and, in a moment, they disregarded her just the same. Angie exhaled and glanced at Andrew; he hadn't noticed the exchange. He grinned, half a lip curled upward.

"Lively crowd, eh?"

He huffed when she ignored him, instead striding to a particular table in the back beside a door that led down a shadowed corridor. She knew this table. Sitting, she rubbed her hand over its top, smoothed after years of use except for the scarred nicks and grooves won with age. It had seen laughter, and anger, drinks with friends, overheard whispered secrets in illicit liaisons, borne witness to friendships, betrayals, deals, and heartbreak. She knew this table well. Andrew, pulling up his chair, leaned to her ear:

"Why do we have to wait here? Why don't we just ask?"

Angie removed her hat and ran fingers through her hair.

"This is how it is," she said.

"Seems a bit moronic, if you ask me…"

Angie shifted an eye toward him. He cleared his throat and sat up.

"Not that I object, of course," he said.

"Of course."

"Considering the rest of what this place looks like, I'm surprised there's anyone here at all," he said.

"About the only watering hole around," Angie said. "That, and if my memory is right, the railroad should be coming through tomorrow. They only stop here once every few months nowadays, so I'd imagine it would draw a crowd."

The conversation might have continued had it not been for the timely interruption of a woman. Younger, though closer to Angie's age than Andrew's, and lithe, certainly a handsome woman by most measures, exaggerated by how tightly she wore her simple wool dress. Her lips and her bosom were full, her hair red (though obscured by the handkerchief she wore) and eyes struck in an unhesitant way that bore into your own. She caught

Andrew's attention immediately, his mouth curved into an open smile that reminded Angie of the dumbstruck expression of an imbecile. The woman placed one hand on the table, a second on her hip, and leaned slightly.

"Nice to see you back in town, Mrs. Grissom."

"It is good to be back, Courtney," Angie said.

Courtney Walford smiled. She was the daughter of the saloon's owner, a man who at one time was somewhat influential amongst the territorial government. Mr. Walford had been not only the proprietor of the saloon, but also made a small fortune from the copper trade in town, going so far as to serve as the town's representative in the territorial capital. He was personal friends with the old governor and had been a regular amongst the social gatherings of the territory's better-off. For a time, it had been arranged for Courtney to be married to the son of a cattle baron up north, but as Rio del Cobardes' fortunes dissolved so did the Walfords'. Now Mr. Walford was left with nothing but his saloon, and Courtney nothing but a senile old man to tend to. Courtney sat. Their voices descended to murmurs.

"Seen any strangers lately?" Angie said.

"There's at least a couple hiding out in town," Courtney said. "One's a Brotherhood bozo, but I don't know about the other one."

Angie smirked.

"Tell me about him."

"Well, I don't know much," she said. "He's a strange one, that's for sure. Hell, if he didn't dress so fancy he'd probably fade into the crowd, assuming there was a crowd to fade into. Very quiet. Light skin, even lighter hair. His eyes were the color of hazelnuts, wears glasses with these little round lenses. He's kept to himself."

That certainly sounded like her man.

"Not surprising, considering how much is on his head," Andrew said, rushing into the conversation as if realizing he was being left out and needed desperately to be apart. Naturally, it was an octave too loud for Angie's taste. Both ladies glared, Courtney pursing her lips tight and certainly grinding her teeth. Angie shouted vulgarities at him in her mind. He slinked in his chair, but remained transfixed by Courtney.

"Anyway," Courtney said. "Only came in here a couple of times, and was pretty polite too. Bastard didn't leave me a tip either time, though." She chuckled, a deep-throated sound hidden behind a toothy smile. "Cheap scumbag."

Angie smiled too, though stopped short of laughter.

"Catch his name?"

"Something foreign," Courtney said. "Not Mexican, something else. European, maybe.

"Celeron?" Angie said and Courtney nodded, quick and shallow.

"That's it," Courtney said. "But his accent was definitely Easterner, not foreign. I think he sounded sort of like a New Englander. One more thing, I think me might be educated."

"Aren't they all?" Andrew said, risking another interjection.

"No, not the same," she said. "More formal, more highty-toighty."

"What do you mean?"

"Both times he came in here, he started quoting poetry," she said. "I mean, real poetry. Holy Roman, Moorish, English stuff. Not the sort of thing you usually hear miracle workers say. In fact, he sort of reminded me of Mr. Timpson."

Mr. Timpson was Angie and Courtney's schoolteacher. When they were both children they attended classes at his schoolhouse a few miles outside Verdopolis, this before Mr. Walford made his money and Rio del Cobardes fell on hopeless times. Mr. Timpson himself was something of a mystery to Angie: he'd come from back East, Delaware if she remembered right, and had some sort of Ivy League education. She never found out why he left that world to teach little frontier girls and boys reading and writing when he could have, she imagined, enjoyed his twilight years comfortably teaching at a college back east. He'd died well before she was old enough to think of the question, and by the time she did few remembered him at all.

Angie and Courtney had been rather close childhood friends, and were probably the only childhood friend either still spoke too. In Angie's case, Courtney may very well be her only real friend outside business associates like Andrew or Wilson, or family like Joshua. How many people had she lost contact with in the seven years since she started hunting bounties? It wasn't like she was invited to many social functions anymore, not when she'd become a rough and tumble gunslinger while what few friends she'd had as a girl had married and begun families. Except for Courtney. Perhaps they remained close because they were somewhat kindred in outlook: tougher than the average lady, more willing to speak her mind and unafraid to use a pistol if needed too. Angie certainly did, and living in a town that had descended so far into hell had taught Courtney the value of bullets as well.

"You think he's a teacher?" she asked.

"He sounds like one," Courtney said. She rested both elbows on the table and leaned in. "Really, Angie, he certainly does not seem like the sort of man you go for. What did he do?"

Angie smirked.

"He skimped on the tip, that's what," she said.

Courtney laughed and said, "Cheap scumbag!"

Angie laughed too; one of the other patrons glanced in their direction for a moment but just as soon turned away again. At last Angie sighed and composed herself.

"Did the scumbag leave an address?" she said.

+ + +

Andrew flicked aside his spent cigarillo as they stepped through the front door of the Grand Penterson Hotel. There was nothing 'grand' about this god-forsaken place, though, left to rot in the unforgiving sun and forgotten by even those who still foolishly lived here. The establishment was one of the few still alive in this dead town, though only just barely: an old man, the proprietor Angie assumed, looked up from his Bible as the pair stepped in. He didn't so much regard Angie as he did the faint trail of dust she carried in with her, barely noticeable amongst the white sand and gray dust already collecting everywhere. He went back to his book without a word.

Looking to the left, where the old proprietor sat, was what may have been the only other saloon in town, though it clearly had not seen a visitor in quite some time and just at a glance seemed to be running short of good booze. To the right was a lounge: old chairs with faded green cushions arranged in semi-circles around frail little tables. Everything was coated in dust, or dirt, or a dozen other signs of elderly disuse. The only thing that looked used at all, in fact, was the rather large fireplace on the far end of the lounge area: a pile of timbers, clearly harvested from one of the many abandoned buildings in Rio del Cobardes, sat beside the mudbrick hearth. The whole thing was topped off with a slab of slate that served as a decent mantle: three small pictures were arranged neatly along it, one of a young man, another of a young woman, and a third with the two in a posed embrace. Angie did not bother examining any closer, as none of this was their concern. Instead, she walked over to the old proprietor and took a seat at the bar - the stool squeaked as she did so, the old cushion gushing tiny plumes of foggy grime that smelled of sweat and attics.

"What'll it be?" The old proprietor didn't bother looking up from his Bible again.

"Bourbon."

After a moment, the proprietor reached with one hand under the counter and fished out a nearly empty bottle, never bothering to look up as he did so. He placed the bottle down with a hollow thud.

"That's all I've got left," he said. "Feel free to finish it."

"My pleasure," Andrew said. He finished the bottle with a single gulp, punctuated by a pleased hiss.

"Have any guests staying the night?" Angie said.

"A couple." The old proprietor seemed disinterested.

"Any by the name Sambucci?"

The old proprietor carefully turned the page. The Bible seemed as old as he, its spine broken, covers cracked like the parched earth outside, and the slivers of paper inside so brittle they might disintegrate if only you breathed too heavily on them.

"Room six," he said. Angie slid him a silver dollar and stood.

As Angie and Andrew walked toward the staircase in the middle of the room, directly in front of the entrance, the old proprietor whispered:

"Try not to make too much of a mess. I'm an old man. I don't have the strength I used to."

After this moment of hesitation, Angie proceeded forward and up the flimsy "grand" staircase, being sure to avoid the broken step. Looking down the hole, it seemed to descend into nothing but a dark abyss.

The second floor of the Grand Penterson seemed even more disused that the first. Downstairs at least had plenty of windows and light, vestiges of the town's wealthier heyday, but up here was like creeping down a desolate alleyway back in Verdopolis, tinged with the deep red reflections of sunset creeping in from under the doors and the staircase behind her. The hall was long with four doors on each side boasting iron copies of the numbers one through eight nailed into them. Outside the sixth door,

Angie drew her Colt Paterson. Andrew, his LeMat Revolver already drawn, grasped the door's knob.

A breath.

A slight twist of Andrew's wrist, but the brass orb didn't budge. He and Angie shared a glance. He tilted his head. She nodded.

Another breath.

Two steps back, then WHAM! The door flung open and the bounty hunters rushed in, guns raised: the room was small, bathed in deep burgundy and mostly bare, little more than a flimsy looking bedside table and a rather decrepit bed. Angie might have discerned more details had she not been more focused on the lanky man in clerical robes, startled by the sudden intrusion, falling off the bed.

"Celeron Sambucci?"

The man adjusted his glasses and sat up, the bed against his back. His face was pale, but regaining its color. It was a young face, perhaps thirty. He had light auburn hair, soft eyes, and the same small round glasses from the wanted poster.

"Are you Celeron Sambucci?" Angie said. The man glanced at the bedside table, and the thick old tome resting on it - some text of Biblical power, no doubt. He stood, rattled but his resolve growing.

"That would be DOCTOR Sambucci, madam," he said, the words dripping with tones of a posh Boston upbringing and a substantial helping of fear. His hands trembled, but Angie knew from her many encounters with miracle workers to not assume it was from fright. "What do you people want with me? Are you from the

Brotherhood?"

"Do we look like preachers?" Andrew said.

"Either you're incredibly stupid or a downright fool." Angie took one step forward, her Colt Paterson aimed squarely at the bridge of Doctor Sambucci's nose. "You do realize there's a price on your head?"

Sambucci frowned and tilted his head.

"I'm wanted?" he said. "For what? Where?"

"You can sort it out with the Judge back in Verdopolis."

Doctor Sambucci looked from Angie to Andrew and then reached for the old book, meaning to snatch it. His hand snapped back like rubber when Angie's bullet punched a pencil-sized hole into the bedside table. She pointed the Colt Paterson at him again.

"Don't be a fool," Angie said. "Come quiet. My associate here does not often miss this close, and I'm a better shot."

Sambucci's eyes darted between Angie and Andrew once more, then he shut them and began to whisper. In Aramaic. When dealing with a miracle worker, that was never a good sign.

Angie cocked her Colt Paterson.

"I said-"

She was interrupted by the floor disintegrating.

The room and its occupants fell into the hotel's lounge area underneath, Angie landing on her side amidst a shower of splinters ablaze in blue flame. She tossed off a remnant of the bed that threatened to pin her and coughed, choking on the lifetime's worth of dust erupting from every pore and crack in the building. Just as she regained her senses, the hotel was rocked by an explosion - Sambucci had blasted his way through a wall and into the street. Angie stood, spun, and fired twice after him. She missed, although it couldn't have been by much, and with a flap of his robes was gone, vanished amidst a plume of dry sand.

Andrew, bruised but no worse, emerged from rubble.

"Sweet all mighty..." he said. "This is far more trouble than you led me to believe, Mrs. Grissom!"

She sighed, then holstered the Colt Paterson.

"I knew it. I should have hit Wilson when I had the chance."

Chapter Four

Doctor Sambucci's trail went cold quick. If there was one thing Angie had learned after tracking so many miracle workers, it was that once a miracle worker had escaped it was little use giving chase: with their miraculous arts, it was easy for him to cover his tracks or lay down red herrings. Frustrating, but no amount of running or riding in the general direction the bounty had vanished into would do much good. Much better to just call it a day, clean your guns, and try to guess what direction he'd go next.

Back at the Saloon, Courtney had the whiskey already poured and ready. She knew by the expression on Angie's face that things hadn't gone according to plan, and did little more than nod in Angie's direction as she kicked back the shot. Andrew, on the other hand, remained all smiles.

"Darlin', you should've seen it," he said. He was exaggerating his Cajun drawl now, smiling wry and leaning so far over the bar's countertop he may as well have laid on it. Angie rapped fingers on her hip, inching ever so slowly for her Colt Paterson's ivory grip… "It was like the Fourth of July. Pow! Ba-Zoom! A show worth every nickel, had we not been caught up in it. Anyways, so there we was, covered in soot and brimstone and what have you, and the bespectacled miracle worker all fired up – I do mean that literally – and ready for a fight. But did I cower? Nosiree. I was all ready for a fight, but wouldn't you know it? Man was yellow, didn't bother to stay and see things through. Just up and ran."

Courtney played along, though Angie caught the slight roll in her eyes.

"Sounds like you nearly broke your neck," she said, appending it with a small smile.

"Oh, there was never a chance of that," Andrew said. "If so, I'd never been able to make my way back here to enjoy a fine drink from a fine lady. And as Mrs. Grissom here will testify, there's not much that can stand in my way on that matter."

Angie sighed, shook her head, and turned away. The saloon was dead now: the aged wood and piles of dust in the shadowed corners gave the appearance of an abandoned shell. With Rio del Cobardes nearly dead itself, it was no wonder the nightlife had perished. Other than Andrew, Courtney, and herself, the only other soul was old Mr. Walford, tucked away upstairs someplace lost in the memories of his former wealth.

Angie called an early night and made her way into the backside of the Saloon, which at one time doubled as an inn but in recent days was little more than ample closet space. Courtney had cleared out one room while they were off sparring with Sambucci: a couple of small beds were fitted with relatively fresh cotton sheets and some rattier blankets, a small kerosene lamp left on a box in the corner made for a makeshift nightstand. Good enough. She hung her coat and hat on a nail jutting out of the door's back, and left her boots in the corner. Rather than sleep, Angie disassembled and cleaned her revolvers, counted her bullets, and thought over what steps they should take next.

Angie also counted the nights. The night after next would be the Quarter Moon, the night when Andrew's condition would inevitably grow beyond whatever control he had over it and the murderous abomination hiding behind those amber red eyes would be unleashed. It made working with him difficult – nothing got in the way of a job like worrying that your partner was only a night away from a killing spree – but, she didn't trust anyone else to contain the boy without killing him. She'd nearly done so herself on more than one occasion. It wasn't easy, either: he'd need to be shackled and guarded for much of the night, and with the strength his condition afforded him there was always the possibility that the heavy iron chains Angie always brought along would someday give way.

And on that day, she'd have to use the .38 caliber tucked away in the small of her back.

Her thoughts wandered back to their bounty, Doctor

Sambucci. Where could he be now? She didn't believe he
could've gotten far with nightfall and miles of desert in all
directions. She could picture him now, skulking through
the darkness of the town. He'd stick to the narrow passages
between buildings, and closer to those that looked nearer
collapse. Anything with light was, of course, to be avoided.
There would be faint wafts of sand, sage and burning
timber on the wind. At last he'd settle on a house that
looked suitably abandoned, but not quite in total disrepair.
He would consider using some holy power to make an
opening, but would in the end decide against it. Instead,
he'd use a mere mortal rock to smash open a door. Inside,
the house would be lathered in healthy layers of dust, but
still furnished. The previous owner would probably not
have bothered to take anything with him when he left:
maybe some rotted food remained in the pantry, and she
imagined clothes that smelled of stale wood hanging in the
bedroom. The good doctor, a snobby Easterner, would
recoil at this peon's hut, but would swallow his pride. He
needed a place for the night.

Andrew and Courtney continued their banter for
some time, it seemed, as Andrew didn't turn up until well
after all of that. He seemed surprised when she turned to
face him, lying in bed still fully clothed (as she so often
slept).

"You're still awake?" he said. Angie watched as he
squirmed a little. After a moment or so, she whispered:

"She's no harlot, dog-boy. She'll skin you alive."

Andrew laughed. He undressed to his long johns -
Angie had no qualms sleeping in the same room with a

nearly naked man, not when she thought of him more as boy than an adult.

"Aw, don't be so harsh, Angie," he said. "She can't be that bad."

Angie sighed. The Cajun was thick-headed: he saw most women as merely cattle he could woo to bed and conquer. His natural charm and friendly nature made it easy for him to place many under his spell, though granted the vast majority of that "many" were harlots who'd sleep with any man who named the right price. But Courtney was different. Angie ground her teeth.

"I warned you." The words came out more as a hiss. "Don't be stupid."

Andrew sat on the bed, backside to her. When he said nothing, Angie decided to roll over and try for some sleep. Eventually, in the dark, he whispered:

"She's not the same. Courtney's different. Not sure how."

And that's all that was said.

Later that night, Angie was stirred out of her sleep by soft noises wafting in from elsewhere in the otherwise silence. Even in the state between sleep and wake, it wasn't difficult to make out the soft moans, grunts, and sighs. One glance at the empty, barely touched, bed beside her told her enough. After that, she was in too foul a mood to sleep, but at some point did so and dreamt of riding, of fighting, and her husband's funeral.

+ + +

Andrew, still half-naked, returned to their room

around dawn to find Courtney already awake, already roused, and carefully loading cartridges into her Colt Paterson. He froze in the doorway. Perhaps he thought she'd finally had enough his antics and intended to gun him down right there? Angie might've laughed at the thought had she been in any mood to.

"Oh," he finally offered. "Mornin', Mrs. Grissom."

Angie snapped the revolver shut with a metallic clack. She glanced at him, then holstered the gun.

"Get dressed."

He nearly dived out of the way as she strolled out the door. Breakfast was eggs, biscuits and stale water - the best Courtney could manage. They sat at the saloon's bar and chatted over the meal, reminiscing their childhoods and laughing over some of Angie's more recent adventures. Andrew didn't come up - Courtney was smart enough not to mention it, and Angie valued their friendship too highly to make it an issue. Besides, it wasn't Courtney she was upset with.

Andrew emerged mid-morning as if nothing had occurred, took a seat two stools away, and immediately struck up a conversation with Courtney. Unlike the night before, her responses weren't coupled with eye rolls but seemed instead rather genuine. Whatever powers Andrew Carnation had over the opposite sex, even a lady as hardened as Courtney Walford wasn't immune.

For a moment, Angie imagined herself in Courtney's place: happy, if only a little; in love once more. She imagined Uncle Josh so happy, worries about money and her livelihood gone for good. She could be married, she could have children, maybe move back east. But, not before visiting Elijah's grave one last time and placing the Colt Paterson on his tombstone…and there, the daydream crumbles. Angie's life with Elijah floods back to her: their wedding and the night, that blissful year after, the day the Sheriff's deputy arrived with news of his murder, the tears and, at last, the rage. The rage that drives her to keep on shooting, the last tangible thing left of him.

Angie was about ready to break up the love birds when the front swung open and in plodded an old man with sunken eyes, bald head, a wide gut, and white beard. He wore ragged old boots, while his blue shirt was dirty and unbuttoned. Courtney sprinted to his side and led him to a seat.

"Did you enjoy your walk this morning, Papa?" she said.

Old Man Walford mumbled a response.

"Oh, them?" Courtney said. "It's Angie, Papa. Angie Grissom. You remember Angie. We went to her wedding."

He mumbled again, this time coupled with a nod, and clutched a ragged tablet to his half-bare chest. No…not a tablet. A book. Angie stood.

"Court, what does he have there?"

Courtney took the book from her father - it slid from his arms effortlessly. Angie was now certain: it was the book Doctor Sambucci had on the nightstand in his hotel room. Courtney opened it and flipped through a few pages, but then seemed perplexed.

"Papa, this ain't even in English," she said. "Where'd you find this thing?"

"Probably at the Grand Penterson," Angie said as

Courtney passed the book to her. It was old, older than any book she'd ever seen before, and completely covered in meaningless handwritten scribbles. It could be a language, but none that Angie was familiar with. The lettering was fancy: strange swirling characters written with an eye toward calligraphy. In the margins were drawn bizarre, almost demonic, figures - creatures with three heads and twenty-seven limbs, or seven wings on what otherwise looked like a rolled-up hedgehog. She flipped the page: there was a diagram of some kind pictured, a strange and enormously complicated symbol. The pages were yellowed and ragged, and the whole book was as large as a Bible though not nearly as heavy. There was a lock embedded in the dust laden satin cover, engraved in the some of the same mysterious symbols that lined every page, but the latch had broken at some point

"What is it you have there?"

A stranger entered the saloon. He was a tall broad shouldered man in his late forties or early fifties, his thick black hair graying at the edges. He wore a miracle worker's robes, and a large crucifix hung from his neck. He was dark skinned, though light enough to perhaps be a mulatto. The man did not smile.

"Oh, this old thing?" Angie said, flipping it shut and resting it under her arm. Her free hand rested on the Colt Paterson. "Just doing some light reading. One-Thousand and One Arabian Nights. You know, re-familiarizing ourselves with the old classics. Haven't read this stuff since we were schoolgirls. You know how it is."

The man swiveled his jaw as if he were gnawing on

something.

"Give it to me," he said. His voice was baritone and filled with venom, the voice of a man used to getting what he wanted as soon as demanded. His dark brown eyes were fixed on the book.

"Excuse me?" Angie said. "Not very well mannered for a miracle worker, are you? The name's Grissom. And you are?"

The miracle worker squinted his eyes, but did stand a tad taller.

"I am Thaddeus Cleomente, loyal servant of his holiness Chovis Rhinewald, Abbot of Montpelier," he said. Angie exaggerated a nod. Courtney strolled back to the bar and poured herself a drink.

"Oh, I see, you're a man of the Brotherhood," Courtney said, downing the shot without pause. "Out to liberate the downtrodden frontiersmen from under the thumb of the elite?"

Brother Cleomente's eyes shifted to Courtney for only a moment, then returned to the book.

"You have no idea what it is you are holding," he said. "Give me the book, or I will take it from you."

"Is that so?" Angie said. She drew the Colt Paterson and aimed for the wide bridge of Cleomente's nose. "I've met miracle workers who could stop bullets, and a couple who could pull this here gun from my fingers with a mere thought. What, sir, can you do? Better yet, what can you do with two guns pointed at you?"

At the bar, Andrew swiveled around on his stool, LeMat revolver already drawn and already aimed.

"Hadn't thought you'd noticed, ma'am," he said.

"Mr. Carnation, I know you better than anyone," Angie said. She pulled back her revolver's firing hammer. "Just as well as I know that Mr. Cleomente here is going turn around and forget all about this silly old book."

Brother Cleomente grimaced.

"I did not come to fight you," he said. "But, I must have that book. It is imperative I have it. You have no idea the danger it represents."

"Then perhaps you should have thought of that before making threats," Angie said. Without another word, Brother Cleomente left. She sighed and took a step back, holstering the Colt Paterson again.

"Hoo-eey," Andrew said, making a bit more of a show of his relief. "You alright, Miss Walford? I hope the excitement wasn't too much for you. Tends to happen quite a lot when Mrs. Grissom's around."

"Nah, darlin'," Courtney said, pouring herself another drink. "You two are the most that's happened here since the town up and died."

Chapter Five

There wasn't much left of the Grand Penterson Hotel when Angie and Andrew returned at noon. The damage caused by Doctor Sambucci the evening before had been the final straw for the crumbling relic, and over the night most of the building had collapsed. Now little remained except a mountain of broken timbers that smelled of rotten oak, dust and sulfur. As Andrew lit a cigarillo, Angie surveyed the scene - keeping an eye out for the old man they'd briefly met the day before. Nothing. What could have become of him? Old man Walford was too senile to tell them anything useful. A man that far along into his twilight, tending to an abandoned hotel in a dead town all by himself with nothing more than a Bible and liquor to keep him company... where would a man like that go after all that was taken away? The thought passed away, and Angie focused on the task at hand: finding some hint to where their bounty had run off to or, short of that, any idea where Celeron Sambucci would go next.

"Though, I'll be damned if any useful clue managed to survive in this mess," she said. Andrew laughed, a puff of tobacco smoke blasting from his lips.

"You're quite the optimist, today, Mrs. Grissom." He waded into the wreckage, dry wood and shattered plaster crunching under his boot. Tucked under his arm was the odd book Old man Walford had found. Angie snatched it from him.

"Why did you bring this thing along?" she said. Andrew responded with a shrug. With a sigh of surrender, Angie handed it back to him. They turned toward the debris that approximated Doctor Sambucci's hotel room, just in time for the miracle worker himself to emerge from behind what remained of the main staircase.

Sambucci froze. Andrew dropped his cigarillo. Angie blinked.

Angie had been doing this for quite a long time before this moment. She'd hunted plenty of miracle workers, and thought she'd gotten to know their ilk fairly well. Those who got themselves caught up in the sort of trouble that required her services often fell into a particular pattern: commit some heinous act, flee to an almost forgotten corner of the West, then meditate and pray for some sort of absolution. Upon being discovered, they'd put up a fight - should they escape he'd run off to another forgotten corner. Usually, they'd leave some clue behind, some seemingly insignificant scrap of nothing that Angie had proven quite adept at turning into a general direction (or, short of that, she had a talisman or two that could do that for them).

In seven years, she'd never stumbled upon a bounty so soon after their escape.

"You...you took the Codex!" Sambucci said. He took a step toward them. Angie drew her Colt Paterson. Andrew, one handed, aimed his Winchester rifle. Sambucci took two steps back, seemingly surprised, but then recomposed himself somewhat and pointed at Andrew.

"Give me the book," he said. "Please!"

"Seems this old thing has become the object of everybody's desires," Andrew said. He held the old book up for Sambucci to see. "Way I reckon, you got two choices. You can either surrender yourself quietly and I can hand this over in a friendly manner, or you can be a difficult bastard and make me shoot you."

"I'll be honest, Mr. Carnation," Angie said, cocking back the firing hammer on the Colt Paterson. "After last night I'm preferring that second option."

Sambucci gulped and adjusted his glasses. He appeared overall disheveled: his clothes were streaked with dirt, his pants' right leg was torn, and his bowtie was undone. Unlike most miracle workers she'd encountered who usually dressed in robes or other vestments, Doctor Sambucci was dressed like a fine upper class gentlemen. Or, at least one who'd survived a building's collapse.

"Why...that's blackmail!" he said. Angie rolled her

eyes. Sambucci blabbered on: "You have no right! The book is…is mine! You have no idea how important it is to my research, to my career, to my discipline…"

"Nor do I particularly care," Angie said. "You heard our terms. What's your answer?"

Sambucci glanced from the book, to Angie, to Andrew, to the Colt Paterson. He seemed to be working out something, a counter-proposal perhaps.

Then, the remainder of the staircase decided this was the perfect moment to collapse.

A couple tons of rotten timbers tumbled over, splintering, spitting up the Grand Peterson's last plumes of dust. It was enough to distract the bounty hunters for a moment. A moment was all the miracle worker needed to use his power and, thanks to Andrew's loose grip, snatch the book from the Cajun's hand.

"Feet pue tan!" Andrew cursed and fired the rifle, but one handed and half-blinded, he never stood a chance of hitting. "You goddamned son of a bitch!"

Doctor Sambucci had made a run for it and into the square that marked the center of Rio del Cobardes: a wide area flanked by boarded up shops, presided over by a long since broken down steepled clock tower at the top of what had once been a bank. In the center, surrounded by the dried husk of what had once been a nicely pruned grass lawn, was an old pavilion. It was missing some tiles from its roof, but otherwise seemed to be in the best condition of anything in sight.

Angie stormed after the miracle worker, and she could hear Andrew chasing after only a few paces behind. The moment all three were in the square, however, an immense gust of wind suddenly struck: the sand at the edges of the square began to swirl in immense clouds of dry dust, spinning round and round, forming an immense whirlwind that effectively sealed them inside. Angie and Andrew slid to a halt.

"Sweet Jesus," Andrew said. The walls of sand billowed and boiled angrily around them, roaring as if a train were thundering past, yet there remained not a cloud in the sky. Angie knew at once this was the work of a miracle worker, but never before had she seen anyone wield the Power of God on such a grand scale. She shot a glance at Doctor Sambucci: he appeared just as astounded. That left only one possibility.

"Professor Sambucci. We meet at last."

Thaddeus Cleomente rose from his seat within the pavilion, slow and deliberate, his eyes fixed on Celeron. His face remained the cold grimace he wore when confronting Angie back in the saloon. Celeron, arms still wrapped tight around the book, took a step back.

"You," he said. "You were in the Saloon. You are from the Brotherhood."

"Indeed," Thaddeus said. "Do you know who I am?"

"By name and reputation," Celeron said. "You are Chovis Rhinewald's lackey, his Knight Templar."

Thaddeus stepped out from beneath the pavilion. Every movement was slow, deliberate, non-threatening. Yet, his tone and expression…

"I suppose you could call me that," he said. "The Abbot has communed with God through the archangel

Michael, and unto me passed the holiest of tasks. I merely do as God commands. As a man of the cloth, I am sure you understand."

"I am not a clergyman," Celeron said. There was a particular venom in his voice. "I am not you."

"No, you are not." Thaddeus' grimace became a sneer. "You insult God by questioning the nature of the miracles he has so graciously given us the gift to perform, and even now you stand before me an arrogant boy seeking answers to mysteries that do not need to be solved. A scientist I can forgive, for he seeks simply to reveal the majesty of God's creation. You? You seek to understand the very nature of divinity itself. For what end? What do you hope to do with that power once you have unlocked it?"

Celeron, fury burning behind his little spectacles, wagged a finger at Brother Cleomente.

"Don't you dare lecture me on how to use the Power of God!" he said. "How many countless lives have the denominations taken in the name of God, using the very powers Christ used to cure the sick and uplift mankind? Even just here, in the frontier, where the Brotherhood and the Order have waged their blood feud? You use the Power of God to commit murder, to break the first commandment God put to stone!"

"Yet after all your invective, you never answered my question, Doctor." Little bolts of electricity began to arc between the miracle worker's fingers. "What do you intend to do once you know? What is the purpose of your quest?"

After all that, it seemed Doctor Sambucci could not articulate a real answer.

"You will not lay a hand on the Codex," he at last managed. "I will not let Rhinewald have it."

With a flick of his wrists, two sparkling fireballs ignited in Brother Cleomente's palms. He began to approach Celeron, grim and unblinking.

"Then may God have mercy upon your soul," he said. "You will not leave here…"

BANG!

Thaddeus stopped in his tracks. Both of the miracle workers looked toward Angie as she pulled back the skyward raised Colt Paterson's hammer again.

"Now, now, boys, let's not get ahead of ourselves, shall we?" she said. Andrew already had his Winchester aimed square at Brother Cleomente's temple. Angie walked toward Doctor Sambucci, while keeping the distance between herself and Thaddeus wide. He followed her with his eyes. She kept her pistol drawn on him.

"A woman gunslinger," he said. "Who are you?"

"None of your concern," she said. Celeron seemed unsure what to do when she reached him. "Now, step back from the good Doctor before my associate and I blow your Goddamned head off."

Thaddeus held back a laugh.

Angie grabbed Doctor Sambucci's arm and yanked him along as she began her way back to Andrew.

"I said, take a step back!"

Then, the whirlwind halted. The square was overcome by a sandstorm as the walls surrounding them collapsed. Amidst this, all Angie could see was Thaddeus lunge.

Thaddeus Cleomente sailed through the plummeting

mountain of dust toward Doctor Sambucci, so fast that
Angie had no time to pull the trigger before he was already
atop them. The miracle worker's energized fist slammed
into Celeron's tome, but some force, a miracle the good
Doctor had cast no doubt, reacted to the attack with a
bright flash. Both men were tossed away from each other.
Angie fired at Brother Cleomente, but between the flash
and the cloud her shot missed wide. Both miracle workers
vanished into the sand storm. She was blind.

Then, the light show began: fireballs, bright enough to
pierce the haze, began soaring at random as the miracle
workers began their duel. One fireball flew past Angie, who
had to dive out of the way to avoid being melted to death
by the miniature sun. It slammed into a wall she had not
noticed was only a few paces away, erupting in a blast of
wood and flame. The sound of a building collapsing
heralded a new plume of debris added to the cloud.

She heard the Winchester bark. A fireball flew in the
direction from which it had echoed, but a Cajun curse after
the resulting explosion assured her Mr. Carnation had
survived. She fired a shot at the invisible source of the
attack, it responded with another fireball tossed at her - by
the time it struck, she'd already moved.

A new gust of wind, and the haze began to clear. The
square was pockmarked with flaming black craters, and the
pavilion had been obliterated by an errant blow. Andrew
had somehow ended up on the opposite end of the square,
Celeron was now on her left rather than right. Brother
Cleomente was nowhere to be seen. Angie waved to get
Andrew's attention, then signaled him to keep his eyes

open. She snapped open the Colt Paterson and reloaded.

"Doctor Sambucci," she said, sliding a bullet into its chamber. "I understand you are in the middle of a quarrel with this fellow, but just so the air is clear and there's no unfortunate accidents, please keep in mind that Mr. Carnation and I mean you no considerable harm. Your bounty specifically stipulates that you be delivered to the courthouse in Verdopolis alive." She snapped the Colt Paterson shut and pulled back the hammer. "I care not for whatever doctrinal dispute has brought you and Cleomente to blows, but so long as you insist on continuing this brawl we will stand by you."

"Wait, we will?" Andrew chimed in from across the way. Angie glared. "Oh. Oh, yes, of course! Whatever you say, ma'am."

His breath at last caught, Celeron cleared his throat.

"I…I think I understand."

Angie heard wood creak. She spun toward the bank, gun drawn, and spotted Brother Cleomente, both hands steaming due to the balls of energy building in his palms, standing on top of the clock tower.

"Why are you getting yourselves involved in this business, gunslingers?" he shouted. "You're no better than the Keeper! None of you understand the forces you are meddling with, the danger-"

He is interrupted by a staccato of gunshots as Angie and Andrew opened fire. They miss, the miracle worker stepping behind the clock tower. A moment later, the whole tower lurched toward Angie and Celeron.

"Oh damn…!" was all Angie could say.

Suddenly, an invisible force seized hold of Angie and threw her through the air, sending her tumbling head over heels to safety as the tower slammed to the earth in a thunderous rattling thud. Angie, dizzy and disoriented, didn't realize she had survived until Andrew was already at her side.

"Angie! Good lord, that was close. Are you okay?"

She coughed as she sat up.

"Where's my hat?"

Only after the bowler was resting on her head again did she notice that Cleomente and Sambucci were at it again: Thaddeus, leaping long-ways over the fallen clock tower, threw two more fireballs at Celeron. The good Doctor rolled, one crashing into the sandy dirt beside him while the other soared past his face and into the dirt a yard away. Doctor Sambucci attempted to leap away, but Thaddeus used the same invisible force that had only moments ago saved Angie to throw Celeron to the earth again in mid-flight.

"Give. Me. The Codex!" Thaddeus said, another fireball igniting in his palm. With his free hand, Celeron tossed one at his opponent - Thaddeus swatted it away.

Andrew fired his Winchester at Thaddeus, who swatted the bullet away as easily as he had the fireball and threw another in the bounty hunters' direction. Andrew cursed as he and Angie dove out of the way - he rolled, shouldered the rifle again and fired two more rounds. Thaddeus swatted those away as well and lunged at Andrew, who side stepped the attack, swung the Winchester and clubbed the miracle worker in the jaw.

"INFIDEL!"

Thaddeus pounded an open palm into Andrew's chest, shoving him several yards backward and through the window of an abandoned apothecary. The miracle worker turned his attention to Angie in time for her to throw a fistful of sand into eyes. As he reeled, she swung again and smacked the butt of the Colt Paterson against his head, drawing blood. She tried to follow it with a kick, but even stunned and half blind Thaddeus was able to use a miraculous force to push her away, nearly knocking into Doctor Sambucci's legs as she slid across the square.

"Damn you, woman." Thaddeus wiped the sand from his face, bright red blood now smeared his brow and cheek. Angie rolled onto her stomach and took aim, but did not fire. The miracle worker stood tall, patted the dust from his robes, and grimaced. He turned away, almost as if he had forgotten the battle they were in the middle of. "This is not over, Doctor Sambucci."

Angie blinked. He was gone.

"What in the world..." she said, standing. Brother Cleomente was nowhere in sight. She ran to the spot where he'd stood: nothing remained except for his shoe prints. "What just happened? Where did he go?"

"My God," Celeron said. He seemed pale. "Instant transportation, the ability to appear in one place and then another a moment later...the last person to perform that miracle was Saint Alphonsus of Ligouri, over a century ago..." He hugged the book, the "Codex" as he and Brother Cleomente called it, to his chest. "Cleomente can wield powers on par to the Apostles themselves...!"

A chill ran down Angie's spine. If he was that powerful, then Brother Cleomente could have killed them any time he wanted. This entire fight was merely him toying with them.

"Mr. Carnation!" Angie swallowed her fears. "Andrew! Get your damned ass out here!"

The front door of the apothecary shattered, and Andrew stumbled into the square.

"Anything broken?" Angie said.

"Just filthy and bruised, Mrs. Grissom," he said. Angie turned to Doctor Sambucci, her gun still drawn but not aimed at him.

"Doctor…" she said. He ignored her, lost instead within his own thoughts, eyes more or less turned to the ground but not seeming to look at anything in particular. "Mr. Sambucci!"

Celeron jumped, startled. He took a breath and clumsily adjusted his eye glasses.

"Y-yes? Mrs….ah…"

"Grissom."

"Oh, oh, yes. Of course."

She paced toward him.

"We still have business to attend to, Doctor."

He attempted a brave face.

"Yes…yes, of course," he said. He stood a bit taller, and took on an aristocratic air. "The supposed 'price on my head'."

Angie had halved the distance between them.

"Thirty five dollars, to be precise."

"Ah, yes, I can see now why you and your, ah,

associate would be interested, as I would imagine that is quite a hefty sum for ladies and gentlemen in your line of work…" Celeron said.

"Oh, the deal was sweetened, but thirty five dollars is nice enough on its own," Angie said.

"…And, if I properly understood our brief exchange a moment or so ago, you will not be paid if I am harmed?"

"Killed, more specifically," Angie said.

"Ah." He pursed his lips and looked away. The two were face to face now. He raised his head and wagged a finger, as if just that moment having come to a brilliant conclusion. It was a show, Angie was sure. "In that case, considering that whatever crime I have been charged with in this 'Verdopolis' is surely a mistake on the part of the local authorities, and further considering that the last few minutes seem to indicate that I am in need of some personal protection, perhaps the best course of action is that I go along with you, peacefully…"

Angie smacked her lips.

"Indeed."

Chapter Six

Screeching, a mother falcon glided to a rest on a crag. Her perch overlooked miles of desert, a menagerie of canyons, hills and sand. There was no breeze, and her yellow beak was opened wide as she panted to battle the heat. Everything in sight was baked golden brown and burning to touch. With a flutter of feathers, she was aloft again. The falcon caught an updraft and flew high, above the butte's flat peak, and watched with disinterest as Thaddeus Cleomente appeared from nothing.

The first thing Brother Cleomente saw was blue. Then, he was bathed in the scent of wildflowers.

The mother falcon screeched one last time, then sailed off for places unknown.

Thaddeus stepped forward and placed his precious

cargo on a wide flat stone - a natural altar - and beside it placed the essentials needed for the ritual: a vial of holy water, incense and frankincense, oil and slivers of silver. Inside their cage, three starlings chirped. He closed his eyes, took a breath, and drew a rosary. After counting the beads three times, he kissed the crucifix and held a hand over the birdcage.

"Lord," he said. "Extend your hand over these little beasts and imbue them with the Holy Spirit, grant them the clearness of mind and the fidelity of heart that you have so graciously granted the Men you have seen fit to cast in your Divine image. Bless them with your grace, your kindness, and your resolve. Look over them, now and always."

Thaddeus opened his eyes. The three little birds had gone silent, their eyes all fixed on him. He struck a match, lit the incense, and blew its smoke over them. The transformation had begun.

"Amen."

+ + +

Verdopolis was a bit more than a day's ride by motorcar from Rio del Cobardes, and with the full moon coming up fast Angie was keen to get back before then. Doctor Sambucci's cooperation was both helpful and unique - she'd never had a miracle worker agree to surrender without placing him under some measure of duress. Then again, she'd never hunted a miracle worker who was being chased by a man as powerful as Brother

Cleomente, nor a miracle worker who seemed better suited to a classroom than the desert of southeast Arizona.

They returned to Courtney's saloon and gathered their things, not that there was much to gather, and readied the motorcar. Doctor Sambucci sat quietly in the Model N's back seat, leafing through the old book that seemed to be the center of his troubles, mumbling to himself every so often. As she fished a crank from the trunk and prepared to wind up the motor, Angie wondered whether this man was really worth the thirty-five dollar reward posted. He could be dangerous, sure, but didn't seem quite so...criminal. Courtney was right to compare him to Mr. Timpson: Doctor Sambucci was the same man, just with the Power of God at his disposal.

Regardless, the seventy-five dollars Wilson owed for bringing Doctor Sambucci in would be enough to get the bankers off Uncle Joshua's back, at least for a little while longer. There was less than two-thousand dollars left on the mortgage now. Maybe...maybe she didn't have to do this for much longer after all. Uncle Joshua could still work, after all. Perhaps she could put down the gun and get a more acceptable job. Angie sighed, and pushed the thought from her mind. Even if she could bring herself to put down the Colt Paterson, what other job could she do? After seven years of hunting bounties, she didn't know anything else besides riding, gunslinging, and a bit of fast talk. No. Like the dream of falling in love again, ever moving beyond gunslinging seemed like just another fantastic dream. Only a dream.

The Model N sputtered to life with a belch of acrid

smoke from its tailpipe.

"You wait a moment, Doc," Angie said. Doctor Sambucci seemed to ignore her. She turned toward the saloon. "Mr. Carnation! Time to leave!"

No answer. With a grumble, she went inside.

"Andrew!"

Andrew and Courtney stepped away from each other as she stepped through the doorway - Andrew feigning innocence, Courtney appearing somewhat annoyed by the interruption. Angie took a breath.

"In the motorcar. Now."

"Yes, ma'am!" Andrew said, quick to answer. He turned to Courtney, tilted his hat, and flashed that trademark Southern smile. "Miss Walford, it's been a pleasure."

"Likewise," Courtney said. As soon as he was out the door, she approached Angie and spoke in a hushed tone: "Don't be so hard on the kid. He's sweet."

They embraced.

"Take care of yourself," Courtney said. "Take care of Andy too."

Andy? It'd barely been a day since the two met. Mr. Carnation's charms truly were something to behold.

"I will."

After the first hour had passed, Andrew's courage and chattiness returned. When Angie proved uninterested in conversation, he turned his attention to the miracle worker they toted in the back seat.

"So, what exactly are you doing out here?" Andrew said. "You're no frontier preacher, that's for sure."

Celeron glanced his way, but only for an instant.

"Oh, I see, it's a secret. No hints? I'm not too smart, but I have enough upstairs to know some fancy-talkin' New England miracle worker ain't goin' to travel way out to the Mexican border for no good reason."

"Philosopher," Celeron said. His voice was flat.

"Until you say otherwise, same thing to me. I ain't got a fancy Eastern education."

Doctor Sambucci sighed. He watched the sand and cacti speed by them.

"I study miracles," he said. "I look at them from a naturalistic point of view and try to explain the mechanics. The Church simply decrees that the power stems directly from God."

"Doesn't it?" Angie said. Sermons from her childhood began to wander back into memory from the fog her mind had buried them behind.

"That's what I and my fellow Philosophers want to find out," Celeron said. "The Church holds that Christ taught the Apostles how to perform miracles, and that that knowledge has been passed down amongst the Clergy ever since. When the Schism occurred, that knowledge spread from the Church to the other denominations, including the Brotherhood and this group the locals here call the Order. But all this while, the Clergy has never questioned how they are able to do any of this."

One particularly fiery sermon came to mind.

"You sound like a scientist," Angie said.

Doctor Sambucci smiled. He seemed to take that as a compliment.

"Think of me as a child of knowledge and faith," he said, "I pursue both in my quest for wisdom."

"And this 'Codex' thing…how does that fit in?" Andrew said, tapping the tome resting on the Philosopher's lap. Celeron pursed his lips, and moved the Codex out of Andrew's reach. "Ah, I see. Lips locked right up again, eh? Well, I heard that you stole it from a couple of old monks out in the Sangre de Cristo Mountains. Some sort of Holy relic, eh? What would a stuffy professorial type like you want with that?"

"I'm a tad more interested in why a fanatic like Cleomente is after that thing too," Angie said.

Doctor Sambucci clutched the old book a little tighter.

"It…it's not Cleomente who wants it," he said. "It's Rhinewald."

"Who?" Andrew said.

"Chovis Rhinewald, the Brotherhood's founder and leader," Sambucci said. "He calls himself the 'Abbot of Montpelier', but the truth is that he used to be a shoe salesman from Bangor, Maine. One day he disappeared, then turned up again a year later in Vermont claiming to have communed with the Archangel Gabriel and Saint Paul. Never spent a day of his life in either a monastery or seminary school, yet somehow he knew how to perform miracles."

"Just like that?" Angie said.

"He claimed Saint Paul taught him," Sambucci said. "We were skeptical, of course, but nobody could disprove it. He started the Brotherhood, and his preachings on social justice and worker's rights won him a lot of supporters from the downtrodden."

"That's all well and good," Andrew said, lighting up a fresh cigarillo. "But what does that have to do with the Codex?"

Doctor Sambucci hesitated again, but then whatever desire for secrecy holding him back at last crumbled.

"The Codex is the Gospel."

"What?" Andrew said, incredulous.

"Doc, I looked at thing before we went back to the Grand Penterson," Angie said. "That looks like no Bible I've ever seen."

"No, no! Not the Bible, the Gospel. THE Gospel." He opened the Codex and flipped through its pages. "The monks of the Sangre de Cristos believe that this is the original Gospel, the one upon which all other Gospels are based, written by Saint Peter and touched by the hands of Christ himself.

"Sounds a bit too good to be true, Doc," Andrew said. "You believe this fairy tale?"

"I do," Doctor Sambucci said. "This book may contain the secret of miraculous power, its source, and a reason beyond faith for why simple incantations and artifacts can violate all the laws of nature as science understands them."

"So, with that book anybody could perform miracles?" Angie took off her bowler and scratched her head. "What the hell is something so powerful doing way out here? Why isn't that locked up in a vault someplace?"

"The monks had kept it secret, and few believed their story until recently," Sambucci said. "You saw the pages, it's written in some sort of code. Professor Lohengrin, the man who...ah...lent me the Codex, had received permission to study it firsthand and had managed to translate part of it recently. I'm taking it back to Boston so we can finish decoding and study it properly."

Andrew tapped his cigarillo against the door, the ash blowing away in the wind.

"Then what?"

"What do you mean?" Sambucci said. Andrew turned and blew a puff of smoke toward the Easterner.

"After you translate it and study it. Then, what do you do?" Andrew said. "As Cleomente said back in Rio del Cobardes, what's the point?"

Doctor Sambucci stumbled over the question.

"Um…well, there are many applications for this knowledge," he said. "Medicine, for instance."

"And killin', I'd imagine," Angie said. Doctor Sambucci shot her a glare.

"I would never allow my research to be used for such uncivilized purposes," he said. "The Codex's knowledge will be for the betterment of all humanity."

Andrew snorted.

"Sure, Doc. Whatever you say, Doc."

+ + +

The creatures quivered and panted, their bodies' unnatural growths and contortions at last complete. What once were mere birds now stood as creatures half-human, half-beast - transformed, at Brother Cleomente's direction, by the will of God. They were the size of men, now. Though their faces and torsos had come to resemble a man's, their lower halves maintained the avian form. Their arms remained wings, their eyes were still those of sparrows, but their minds were enlightened. The unfaithful might see what Brother Cleomente had done not as a miracle but a travesty, might call these beings abominations. Monsters. Thaddeus only saw converts to the path of righteousness.

He returned to the impromptu altar and retrieved the oil. He blessed it, then dipped a thumb. The three creatures bowed. He approached one and drew an oily cross on its forehead.

"Fabian," he said. "May God be with you."

He did the same to the next.

"Beth," he said. "May God be with you."

Once more, to the last.

"Anne," he said. "May God be with you."

Brother Cleomente returned the oil, and then emptied the last drops of holy water on each creature's head.

Cleomente paused and looked out across the desert, toward the small canyon carved into the desert only a short flight away and at the tiny, almost imperceptible, road that wound along its edge: a little motorcar was kicking up clouds of sandy dust as it travelled. Cleomente tightened the grip on his rosary beads

"The time has come," he said. "Down there, speeding through the desert, is the infernal book the Lord has tasked us to retrieve. Its guardians are dangerous, and not all of you may return from this battle. I pray for your success. May the Lord watch over you, Athletes of Christ."

The three creatures roared, sprinted for the butte's

edge, and took flight.

Brother Cleomente watched them for a moment, then kneeled and began to pray.

+ + +

After miles of mostly flat desert, the road to Verdopolis became more rugged and wound its way through buttes and rocky outcroppings. This region was a pockmarked with little canyons and building-sized mesas - a generation ago, it made a great place for the natives to ambush white settlers. Today, Angie knew, the Indians had been replaced by bandits and outlaws - the remnants of the "wild" frontier not yet squashed by the lawmen as civilization settled in. Angie steeled her nerves as they reached the worst choke-point: the road dipped below one canyon's lip and followed along its wall. On their right side would be sandstone, while on the left was the canyon floor a long ways down.

The motorcar rounded a bend, followed a slight incline, and Angie was greeted by the sight of the canyon once again. It was an immense crevice several miles long, striped with varying shades of red-brown sandstone, and deep enough she was certain no one could survive falling into. At least, not survive in any way worth calling "survival."

Heights weren't an issue for Angie or Andrew, but Doctor Sambucci seemed to be a different story.

"You okay back there?" Andrew said.

Doctor Sambucci slouched in the back seat, breathed

deep breaths, and took great pains to avoid looking toward the canyon's far wall. He loosened his collar and attempted a smile. His face was somewhat pale.

"Yes," he said. "Yes, of course."

"Don't you fret, Doc, the canyon isn't too big," Angie said. "The road only sticks to the edge for a few miles."

The motorcar hit a divot in the road and Doctor Sambucci yelped like a frightened puppy. Andrew laughed, Angie just smiled and shook her head. She glanced at her side mirror for a moment - three big birds, buzzards perhaps, were floating on the wind well behind them. Doctor Sambucci crossed his arms.

"Not very funny," he said. "Men were not meant to be this high."

"Funny thing for a miracle worker - oh, I'm sorry, a 'fee-low-suffer' to say," Andrew said. He sniffed the air for a moment, then glanced at Angie.

"Philosopher." Doctor Sambucci turned into a schoolteacher again. "It's pronounced 'Philosopher'. You know what I meant. I don't appreciate you belittling my worries, sir."

"I meant no offense, Doc." Andrew reached under his seat, pulled out his Winchester, and checked to make sure it was loaded. Angie glanced into the side mirror again - those buzzards were bigger now, closer, flying in a tight V formation.

No. No, those weren't buzzards.

Angie sped up.

"Oh, perfect." Doctor Sambucci was terrible at muttering under his breath. "Just what we need, to go faster."

"Doc, can you oblige me with a small favor?" Angie said. He sighed and forced himself to sit up.

"Fine," he said. "What is it?"

"Could you take a look behind us for a moment?"

She couldn't see his reaction when he turned, but the words that followed convinced her that his jaw may have slackened, his eyes widened, and perhaps he turned just a shade more pale.

"Mother Mary and Joseph," he said. "Are those harpies?"

"Harpies?"

"Half-man, half-bird abominations," Doctor Sambucci said. "Outside sacrilegious attempts at creating chimeras, they should only live in the mountains of Anatolia and the Levant…"

"So, chances are some fool created those things," Angie said. "Perhaps with the intent to do us some harm?"

"I…suppose…"

"I was afraid of that," Angie said. "You know what to do, Mr. Carnation."

Andrew turned in his seat, rested the barrel of the rifle atop the chair's headrest, and fired. Doctor Sambucci, clutching his ears, barked a curse. The harpies broke their formation - two flew high, one dove in low. Andrew fired again, but narrowly missed as the creature rolled to its left. With a couple flaps of its tremendous wings, the harpy was atop them, grasping for the motorcar with its black talons. The motorcar whipped around a sharp bend in the road - the harpy missed, but Andrew's third shot at last hit: the creature screeched as a bullet struck its hip. It pulled away, diving into the canyon.

As the first harpy retreated, the second descended on them - above and slightly behind, but gaining. Andrew fired twice but, between Angie's driving and the creature's acrobatic contortions, missed.

"Pic kee toi!" he said. "Keep still, damn you!"

That's when the first harpy decided to reemerge from the canyon, directly alongside them. Doctor Sambucci pointed and shouted panicked gibberish. Andrew swung to face the creature but barely got off a shot before it flew into them, slamming atop Doctor Sambucci and the back seat. The motorcar tipped to the left, Angie pulled the wheel hard right, and for a terrifying moment it seemed they'd spin over the cliff. Instead, the Model N righted itself and its side slid against the rocks with the shrill notes of tearing metal.

"It's got my arm!" Doctor Sambucci said.

The harpy tried to right itself, but its left wing was caught amidst the tangle of people and seats. Andrew rose first. He belted it in the cheek with his rifle's butt, to little effect. It screeched at him - its wing came free. Andrew hit it again, it responded with a fanged lunge that never connected. Instead, its chest exploded with a plume of smoke and flame, its wings caught the rushing air, and it fell, dead, to the road behind them.

Doctor Sambucci sat up, his jacket's arm shredded but no worse for wear. The stink of sulfur faded quickly.

Even if it hadn't, Angie had little time to consider it before the second harpy - which had been following all the while and only barely missed crashing into the corpse of its sibling - was now close behind.

"Toss a few more of those, Doc!" Andrew said, opening fire again. The harpy was still adept at acrobatics, however, and managed to dodge the onslaught of lead and flame. A nimble creature, it was almost graceful as it avoided a blast of fire to its left or a bullet just past its brow.

Angie slid through another tight curve in the road - she'd have been amazed at not losing control if she had time to think such thoughts - and at last the cliffside's end came into sight.

"We're almost out of here!" she said. Andrew slid down in his seat and began reloading his weapon, behind her Doctor Sambucci panted heavily. Despite his apparent skills, it was clear he was not used to performing so many miracles in a row. He was nearing the edge of his endurance. Angie steered the motorcar through a narrow uphill pass, smashing the front left headlight in the process, and at last emerged once again onto open land. No longer worried about tumbling over the cliff, Angie's boot stomped on the gas pedal. They began to outrun the Harpy.

"That's it! That's it!" Andrew said. He fired a last shot at the Harpy. "That was a mite tense there, wasn't it?"

Angie shook her head and laughed.

"Yes it was, Mr. Carnation," she said. "Nice shooting."

"You weren't even looking," he said, mimicking a child's whine.

Angie jabbed an elbow into Andrew's ribs.

"I don't need to look, and you know it."

Andrew was about to say something more when a third Harpy landed in the road ahead, flapped its wings, and howled at them. Angie tried to swerve out of the way, but it was too late: the motorcar slammed into the creature at full speed. Angie watched as the creatures bloodied body flopped over the motorcar's hood, listened as its ribcage collapsed and bones snapped. Angie smacked her head against the steering wheel and for a moment was dazed - she reawoke with the motorcar nearly toppled, the Harpy crushed, and a pounding headache.

"Andrew..." she said. Andrew just groaned. She kicked the driver's side door open and tumbled out. The world swirled. Angie pulled herself to her feet, glanced at the bloody mess that was once the Harpy, then reached into the back to shake Doctor Sambucci.

Only, he wasn't there.

"Doc!" Angie spun around, hoping he had just been tossed from the car in the crash. "Doctor Sambucci! Where the hell are you?"

That's when she thought to look up, and sure enough there he was: hanging limp in the talons of the last Harpy, flying back in the direction from which they'd come. Angie drew the Colt Paterson and took two wobbly steps before realizing that it was too late - there was no way she'd make the shot at this distance, and even if she could it was a long way down from there. There was no guarantee Doctor Sambucci could save himself from a rather gruesome death at the bottom of the canyon, and by extension grant Wilson an excuse to cheat Angie and Andrew out of their money. Again.

She spat - her mouth tasted coppery.

Andrew, a streak of blood smeared across his face, stepped up beside her.

"Merde," he said. "Now what?"

Chapter Seven

The first thing Doctor Sambucci saw when he awoke was Brother Cleomente's back, kneeling and hunched over in prayer. The last few moments before he lost consciousness played out in his mind and, immediately, it occurred to him that he must have been captured after the horseless carriage had crashed. The involuntary groan he made as he stood caught the attention of the last Harpy, who shrieked alarm to its master. The Miracle Worker, however, did not turn to face his prisoner. Clutched between the creature's talons was the Codex, scuffed and dirty but no worse for wear despite the abuse dealt it over the last few days.

One glance at their surroundings (Sambucci was thankful his eyeglasses had managed not to be lost amidst the pursuit and his capture) revealed they were not anywhere he could simply run from, but rather were atop a tall butte and beyond the small area containing Brother Cleomente, the Harpy, and himself there was only a long fall to the desert floor below. He had no blessed charm or holy relic on his person that could save him from a fall his high, and surely Brother Cleomente would not grant him the time needed to find and translate a helpful passage from the Codex. His heart sunk. He was trapped.

"Cleomente..." Doctor Sambucci said, but was surprised when the Miracle Worker did not acknowledge him. Curious but cautions, Sambucci approached Cleomente. "Brother Cleomente?"

"Beth...Fabian..."

Sambucci circled about Cleomente, and only upon seeing his face did he realize that the Miracle Worker was not deep in thought or prayer, but distraught. He appeared to have been sobbing at length. Only when he could see Sambucci did he acknowledge him, looking toward the Doctor with a pitiful grimace.

"They are dead, both of them. Only Anne survives," he said. He looked at his hands, as the guilty would on bloody palms. "I perverted them in God's name, and now those poor children are dead. It's all my fault."

He looked up toward heaven.

"Beth! Fabian! Forgive me! Oh God, forgive me..." Brother Cleomente suddenly stood and grabbed Doctor Sambucci by his shirt, bearing a frightening smile. "I...I could resurrect them! Yes! The Lord has given me the gift. It would be taxing on my soul, but I..."

Doctor Sambucci pushed him away, disgusted.

"Even your sect wouldn't turn a blind eye to that," Sambucci said. "Do you think yourself God?"

"But...I could bring them back!" Cleomente said, a note of desperation in his words. "I can still save them!"

"Your abominations are dead. Gone," Sambucci said. Part of him sympathized with the Miracle Worker's pain, but his disgust overwhelmed his softer tendencies. His words were cold and stern. "If they had souls at all, then they are now with the Almighty. You have been given a truly extraordinary gift, Cleomente. Do you really want to violate the trust God has placed in you by using His power for such a petty personal matter?"

Cleomente stared at Sambucci, for a moment speechless. He took a breath, stood straighter, and the grief drained from his expression. He now looked at Sambucci more thoughtfully, more like the man the Doctor had met in Rio del Cobardes.

"For one so foolish, you speak the truth," he said. "Death is final, that is a rule all men of the cloth have sworn to respect. Thank you, for reminding me of that."

In that moment, Cleomente's sadness gave way to anger. Sambucci, and even the Harpy called Anne, backed away. Enormous plumes of fire ignited in the miracle worker's palms, the Earth around them shuddered and the stars above began to fade away. His gaze was unfocused, as if concentrating intently on an image in his mind's eye.

"I can see them, the bounty hunters," Brother Cleomente hissed. "They are asleep now around a campfire. It would be no effort for me smite them, and you too, here and now. A bolt of lightning, a geyser of steam, fire from the heavens or maybe evacuate the air around them…"

Cleomente reached out and an invisible force yanked Sambucci through the air from where he stood until his throat was enwrapped by the miracle worker's fingers.

"Most satisfying of all, though, would be to choke the life out of each of you," he said. "Slowly."

Cleomente squeezed, and for a moment Sambucci was certain he would be murdered. The moment passed. Cleomente released him - Sambucci coughed as he regained his breath. The miracle worker took a breath, and calm washed over him. The earthquake subsided and the stars returned.

"No. Vengeance is not justice," Brother Cleomente said. "For me to pass judgment on you would be as great an insult to God as resurrecting my fallen children. I will not sully my hands with your blood."

He looked to the heavens.

"Forgive them, my children," he said. "The Lord already has."

Doctor Sambucci, rubbing his throat, backed away from the Miracle Worker. The man was mad, he was sure of it. He may not murder him today, but there was no telling when Cleomente's dark side would well up again to complete the task.

"What do you intend to do with me?" Sambucci said, his voice still hoarse.

"You know too much about the book and its secrets," Brother Cleomente said. "I had hoped you would give me the book and we would part ways, but now it is clear that is no longer possible - you will never part with it willingly, and if I take it by force you will pursue me in an effort to take it back. You leave me no choice but to take you as my prisoner, at least for the time being. I will escort you back to the Montpelier, where Abbot Rhinewald will oversee the book's final fate."

Doctor Sambucci pointed toward the Codex, still resting in the Harpy's talons.

"Do you truly believe Rhinewald will just destroy the book?" he said. "Do you have any idea what this is, the sort of power you'd be granting him access to?"

"I know that I have been commanded to retrieve it and that the Abbot intends to destroy it," Brother Cleomente replied. "I also know it is a power foolish naive men like yourself cannot be allowed to possess. Anything else is meaningless detail."

+ + +

The Fraternal Order of the Knights of Saint Telemachus, or simply "the Order" as the locals called it, had been established by several prominent miracle workers and clergymen in 1899 as a place where those morally outraged by the Brotherhood could gather in private to discuss liturgical and philosophical rebuttals to the radical upstarts after they had first started to trickle into the territory. In practice, it quickly became banner under which one half of the miniature religious war was fought. Those in the Order enjoyed greater respect and support from the locals, but their tolerance for the violence the Order's members had proven willing to engage in was distasteful to most. What had started innocently enough had, by 1909, descended into lynch mobs and murder.

It was dark by the time Angie and Andrew reached the next town on the road, a nice little place called Arenaroja. Unlike seedy Verdopolis or dead Rio del Cobardes, Arenaroja was a respectable place albeit on the small side - there was little else here besides a few houses, a Post Office, a Saloon, a General Store, and the local law. The quiet, even from the Saloon despite a dim light in the windows, unnerved Angie. No matter, they were not going to stop there anyway. Instead, they marched straight to the large Georgian style house on the far end of town that she'd spotted on their first ride through en route to Rio del Cobardes. Unlike the Brotherhood, whose members chose to live ascetic monastic lives and proselytize, the Order's members maintained a series of meeting houses throughout the territory. Even in the dark, the large hatchet-and-cross seal of the Order, emblazoned above the front door, was unmistakable.

"You sure this is a good idea?" Andrew said.

"I don't see what choice we have," Angie said.

"Well," Andrew said, fishing a fresh cigarillo from his pocket. The flare as the match lit revealed beads of sweat on his brow, and the distinct if muted glow to the reds of his eyes. "We could always go to the Sheriff or the Marshalls."

"And what could they do? You saw what Cleomente was like." Angie, without hesitating any further, strode to the door and banged with her fist. "If anything, we're skipping the middle man."

A slit in the door, just about invisible in the dark, slid open and a pair of dark brown eyes sporting thick brown eyelashes peered through. Considering the quickness of the response, those eyes must have been standing guard on the other side, waiting.

"It is late."

"I want to speak with your Knight Commander," Angie said.

"The Knight Commander is quite busy," said the eyes, their voice rumbled like a distant storm. "Please come back another time."

"Tell him Angela Grissom and Andrew Carnation are here to see him," Angie said. "That'll change his mind."

The eyes narrowed a moment, before the slit slammed shut. Heavy steps plodded away on the other side. Angie looked back toward Andrew: he maintained his faux calm facade, smoking his cigarillo while casually eyeing the windows and corners for gun barrels. Steady stomps from within the Order House heralded the doorman's return. A heavy-sounding deadbolt was undone and the door swung open, revealing a giant of a man: his jaw square, his cheek scarred, and chest barreled. If it weren't for the Priest's collar around the man's neck, he'd look no different than any number of monstrous bandits whose faces adorned the territory's wanted posters.

"The Abbot will see you now."

The giant, not bothering to relieve either of their weapons (although his nose did shrivel at the scent of

Andrew's cigarillo), ushered them in and led them down a hall into a large lounge furnished with armchairs and gentlemen's social tables. Curios, filled with various books and religious artifacts, lined the walls except for the fall wall, which was dominated by a large fireplace. Standing in front of it, a glass of wine in hand, stood the Order's Supreme Commander, a skinny man with a pencil mustache and sharp regal nose: Abbot Ebenezer Moore.

"Merde," Andrew muttered.

Angie knew Ebenezer Moore only through reputation. He was from back East, the third son of a wealthy Virginian family who, for reasons she'd never learned of, had chosen the clergy over material wealth. Not that one could tell just by looking: the man smelt of money. His fine tailored clothes were a league more refined than the niceties of the local rich men. The man was an aristocrat, through and through.

Although not the founder of the Order, he had quickly risen to become their leader within only a couple of years. It was under his leadership that the organization had descended into the band of vigilantes and crooks it had become, all in the name of "defending" the territory from the heretics in the Brotherhood.

"You have some nerve showing your face here, Mrs. Grissom, after what you did to Brother Mills," Abbot Moore said. The doors closed behind Angie and Andrew, and on either side appeared a half dozen more miracle workers, each looking more displeased at their intrusion than the last. Angie eyed the men that surrounded her. She expected this, although it was up to Moore how this would turn out.

"He resisted," she said.

That was not the answer Abbot Moore wanted to hear.

"You shot a man of the cloth!" Abbot Moore said. "In the back!"

A chorus of 'yea's and angry grumbles demonstrated the room's temperament.

"It ain't like I didn't give him fair warning," Angie said. Impotent rage overwhelmed Moore's face and contorted his features into a creature rather unholy in appearance.

"They wanted him alive!"

He threw his glass at Angie, it shattered on the floor in front of her and splattered sauvignon across her boots. Andrew drew his LeMat revolver, the men surrounding them drew a half dozen pistols of their own in turn.

Moore raised a hand and the miracle workers lowered their weapons.

"Please, put away your pistol. There is no need for violence here, I'm sure you recall how to act like civilized people," Moore said. Angie thought of a sarcastic quip, but held back. She looked to Andrew. He nodded and holstered the LeMat. Moore continued: "Why are you here?"

"You heard about the theft up at the Sangre de Cristo Monastery?" Angie said.

"We may have heard something, yes," Abbot Moore said and sighed. He walked to a nearby curio, opened it, and retrieved a new glass which he quarter-filled with more sauvignon.

"Well, we're after the man responsible," Angie said. Abbot Moore took a sip of his wine, and then took a seat in one of the room's armchairs.

"So you intend to put a bullet in this poor gentleman's back too?" he said.

"Oh no, Father, we need him alive," Andrew said. He tapped some ash off the end of his cigarillo, spilling them across the floor. Moore glared at him, but said nothing. "Besides, we've grown a little fond of the four eyed varmint."

"You see, this thief ain't no low down master criminal, he's a mild mannered well to do educated man from back East," Angie said. "After a little persuading…"

"At the end of gun, I imagine," Abbot Moore said.

"…He surrendered peacefully. We were on way back to turn him over to the Law when we were beset by the Brotherhood."

Abbot Moore sat up. The other miracle workers murmured amongst each other.

"Seems the Brotherhood was mighty keen on getting this holy relic, a particularly old book, that our thief stole," Angie said. "So they took him."

Abbot Moore placed his wine down on a social table beside his seat.

"Why are you telling us this?" he said.

"Because the kidnapper was Thaddeus Cleomente," Angie said.

That really got them riled up.

"Rhinewald's dog!"

"Cleomente is here?"

"How did he arrive in the territory and no one know?"

"I take it you folks are familiar with this fellow?" Andrew said. Abbot Moore stood, his grimace was grim.

"Thaddeus Cleomente is Chovis Rhinewald's most valued and most powerful disciple," Abbot Moore said. "If Cleomente was sent to kidnap this thief and steal this holy relic, then no doubt it is imperative he be stopped at all cost."

"I take you boys are going to help us, then?" Angie said.

"How long ago was the thief taken?" Abbot Moore said.

"This afternoon," Angie said.

"He could be anywhere by now!" one of the miracle workers said.

"I was afraid you'd say something like that," Andrew said. Abbot Moore held up a hand again, silencing the miracle workers.

"No," he said. "A relic this important, he would not dare transport it by the usual means."

"I've seen that man vanish from right in front of me," Angie said. "Something called 'instant transportation', I'm told. Could he...?"

"He could, but he won't." Abbot Moore walked to another curio and began leafing through the contents. "No, he's still in the territory, I'm certain of it. He will be holed up in one of the Brotherhood's sanctuaries, preparing a special convoy to transport himself and the book back East. Possibly via a chartered train."

"Any idea where this sanctuary might be?" Andrew said. Moore pulled a scroll from the curio, walked over, and unrolled it atop one of the clear social tables to reveal a map of the territory. Angie and Andrew gathered around.

"There are dozens throughout the territory, he could be at any one," Abbot Moore said, but then pointed to a specific point in the desert south of Laguna.

"If I were to stake my soul on just one, though, it would be on El Abeto Violeta."

Chapter Eight

El Abeto Violeta stood on a teardrop shaped hill, surrounded by a vast barren wilderness. Little surrounded the mission besides sand, ridges dotted with dried out shrubs, and more sand. In the moonlight, it reminded Angie of a storybook castle, complete with crumbling battlements and a steepled watchtower. Angie lowered her spyglass and shot a concerned glance toward Andrew: tonight was the night.

Andrew was pale, sweat beaded on his forehead despite the desert chill, and his eyes were visibly bloodshot. Those red irises seemed to glow in the darkness.

One of the miracle workers, a man they called Brother Bolton, noticed.

"Are you ill?" he said. Andrew drew a small leather

flask and took a swig.

"Nothing a little bourbon can't cure," Andrew said. He offered Bolton the flask, but the miracle worker turned it down and left the Cajun to his own devices. He joined the other members of the Order, who were now gathered prayer and asking God to watch over them as they engaged in battle against the Brotherhood.

There were five miracle workers in the posse. Besides Bolton there were two other minor members of the Order, little versed in the Holy Secrets and unable to do more than cure cuts and bruises. After dealing with men like Brother Mills and Brother Cleomente, it was refreshing to see miracle workers lugging around rifles and six shooters like typical men. Also along was Abbot Moore, who Angie knew through reputation was able to wield much more significant powers, and the giant they had met in Arenaroja who she'd learned was called Brother Johnston. If he was the same Brother Johnston she had heard was in the employ of the Order, then the man was similarly powerful. If Thaddeus Cleomente was Abbot Rhinewald's dog, then Brother Johnston was the Order's equivalent.

Angie ignored them and joined Andrew by the horses.

"You're going to turn," she said, making certain to keep her voice down. She hadn't felt the need to let their newfound friends know about Andrew's condition, but without doing so couldn't force Andrew to stay behind either with drawing questions.

"Is that such a bad thing?" Andrew said. Angie glared.

"You know what I mean," Andrew said. He took another swig from his flask. "You could use whatever muscle you can get."

"I'd rather have a good shot I can rely on than a bloodthirsty mutt I'm liable to have to shoot between the eyes," Angie said. "I'd rather you stayed behind and chained yourself down, like I'd asked. I still rather you stay here."

"No way," Andrew said.

"It wasn't a suggestion."

Andrew took one more swig from his flask, then resealed it and slid it back into his coat pocket.

"In that case I will duly note your recommendation," he said and, his Winchester slung over his shoulder, walked off toward the rest of the posse.

"Dammit," Angie muttered and followed.

As the pair approached, Abbot Moore stood. To Angie, his outfit seemed more suited for a Cardinal preparing to meet the Pope than a man about to get into a shootout, but she supposed every man had the right to choose what he'd wear to his death.

"I do not suppose either of you have a particular stratagem in mind?" he said.

"Well, after taking a gander over the hilltop, a few ideas come to mind," Angie said. The posse gathered around as she knelt and drew a crude map of the mission and its surrounding ground in the sand. "Okay, so the plan as I see it: you boys will draw Cleomente and as many the Brotherhood's miracle workers away from the mission."

"My Brothers and I are not pawns in a game of chess," Abbot Moore said, monotone but with a subtle hint of contempt.

"Father, Mr. Carnation and I are here for one reason only: to recover Doctor Sambucci so we can claim our bounty," Angie said. "Whatever sort of holy crusade you intend to wage out here, that's between you and the miracle workers over yonder. I just suggest you do your duelin' over there instead of over here."

She indicated the places she meant, those being the southwest and southeast sides of the mission respectively. Abbot Moore nodded.

"As I was sayin': you boys draw Cleomente out," Angie said, drawing more lines in the sand. "Mr. Carnation and I will come up this way around the southeast end of this ridge, hopefully without being spotted. We go in, we get our man and the relic, and get out. We will signal you once we are clear, then we'll leave it to you whether or not you wish to continue shooting."

"Do you intend to fight at all?" Abbot Moore said.

"What, exactly, do you expect us to do if y'all can't beat Cleomente?" Andrew said. "We ain't no miracle workers. We ain't even philosophers like Doc Sambucci."

Angie noticed that his voice had become hoarse, and with each following minute he appeared more ill. Andrew had proven once or twice before he could hold back the beast for some time after the full Moonrise, but like a nasty nausea felt coming on throughout the day it was only a matter of time. He would turn tonight, she was sure, it was just a question of when.

"We'll do what we can," Angie said. "If it looks bad, though, we're high-tailing it back to town."

Moore and the other miracle workers did not look pleased.

"Does anyone have an alternative plan? No? All right then," Angie said. She stood and turned to Andrew. "Come on, mutt."

"Wait," said Moore. Angie stopped and turned back toward the miracle workers "The Brotherhood will be holding your thief in the living quarters, on the north end of the mission." Moore raised his hand and made the sign of the cross. "May God be with you."

Angie tipped her hat to him and the two groups separated.

Angie and Andrew made their way along the ridge, keeping low and out of sight. When they reached the ridge's end, southeast of the mission, all sound suddenly ceased. Angie looked to Andrew and tapped her ear, he nodded in agreement. They'd seen miracle workers do this before, somehow silencing the world around them for as far as a quarter mile. It meant the Order was about to begin its attack.

The Mission lit up, and the fireworks began. Fireballs, one or two at a time, landed near the mission's west gate. Considering the distance from the ridge to the Mission, Angie was impressed by the miracle workers' throwing arms. One struck the gate itself, which erupted in flames. It was at then that several men, some dressed in monastic robes and others in plain clothes, burst through the burning gate with Winchesters and Long Rifles.

Sound returned with cracks of gunfire.

Angie, satisfied with the distraction, gestured to Andrew and the pair crossed the miniature valley separating the ridge from the hill, climbing up a barely visible path toward the Mission's east gate.

To Angie's surprise, the gate was unlocked and unguarded. The two slipped inside. Despite the flurry of activity in the Mission's courtyard, all eyes were to the battle erupting at the southwest gate and nobody noticed them. The pair slipped into a little door just to the side of the gate and once again out of plain view.

Inside was a small room, an office of some sort. Angie didn't dwell on it, just ensuring that it was empty before exiting through another small door on the opposite end into long narrow hallway that ran along the Mission's eastern face.

"If Moore ain't lying, this should take us straight to the Doc," Angie said. Andrew, pale and clammy, grinned and bowed.

"Ladies first," he said. Angie couldn't help cracking a little smile. Angie led the way, keeping one eye on the stairwell at the end and the doors that lined the left-hand wall. They had made it about halfway when a door swung open and a Brotherhood goon, wielding a hatchet, charged at Andrew.

"Order scum!" the goon wailed and swung, but Andrew ducked and the hatchet scratched the wall.

"Merde!"

Andrew smacked the butt of his rifle into the miracle worker's belly and pushed him away. The miracle worker swung again and this time managed to slice a bloody gash across Andrew's right bicep. The hall too narrow to raise his rifle, Andrew tried to shoot from the hip but miracle worker grabbed barrel and pushed it away.

Andrew fires into wall. The Brotherhood fanatic

didn't even flinch despite his hand clearly being burnt. Instead, the miracle worker slammed the hatchet's handle against Andrew's temple. The Cajun toppled over.

All of this had happened in just seconds.

"Andrew!"

The miracle worker turned to face Angie, but made it only a step before she put two bullets in his chest. The man stumbled and fell forward. She hopped over the corpse to help Andrew to his feet, but stopped short. Andrew was now convulsing out of control on the floor and drenched in sweat.

"Oh God," she said. "You're turning…"

"Go…" Andrew hissed through chattering teeth. His eyes are blood red with scarlet irises.

"It's a full Moon, you won't be able to control it!" Angie said. She reached for the .38 caliber.

"Go!"

The word was not spoken, it was roared.

Angie knew that she should not leave him, that if there was any time to finally use a silver bullet it was now. Despite that, she let her hand fall away from the revolver. She turned and ran, his screams growing louder as she fled up the stairs.

+ + +

Angie kicked in the door and barely missed being clobbered in the head by Doctor Sambucci, who swung wild as she barged in. He hadn't even finished swinging when she body slammed him into the wall, the muzzle of her Colt Paterson stabbed against the underside of his chin.

"Mrs. Grissom!" he said, dropping the broken chair leg turned impromptu club. "What in blazes are you doing here?"

"Saving you!" Angie grabbed him by the collar and shoved him back into the hall. His glasses fell and clattered against the floor. "Hurry! I've no idea how long the Order can keep Cleomente and the Brotherhood distracted before they notice you're gone."

"No," Doctor Sambucci said, retrieving his glasses. "I can't leave, not yet. Not without the Codex!"

"Doc, we don't have time for this!" Angie said, but the Easterner was unmoved by her impatience and crossed his arms.

"Mrs. Grissom, you've seen what Brother Cleomente is capable of," Doctor Sambucci said. "That book has the power to grant every member of the Brotherhood unrestricted power. Do you really want that?"

Angie wanted to clobber some sense into him, but thinking of it decided that what he said really was sensible.

"…Goddammit," she muttered. "Where is it?"

"I overheard Brother Cleomente order them to place it in the church," Doctor Sambucci said.

"The one on the south end of the Mission?" Angie said. "One quick detour, then. Stay close to me and if anybody starts shooting, you hide. Understood?"

"As you say, Madame."

She led him downstairs, keeping an eye out for men and monsters, and back out into the courtyard. The space was empty now, everyone having either hid or run outside to face the Order's attack. An occasional gunshot would bark in the distance.

"Ah, there it is! See?" Doctor Sambucci said. He would have run off across the courtyard had Angie not grabbed his collar and pulled him back. "What are you…?"

"I don't like it," Angie growled. "It's too open. This could be a trap."

"Mrs. Grissom, you're the one concerned with delaying this rescue," Doctor Sambucci said and pointed toward the church. "And this is the fastest way, I'm sure."

Angie's answer was interrupted by a clap of thunder and an earthquake powerful enough to knock Doctor Sambucci off his feet. A column of fire erupted from the desert to the southeast of El Abeto Violeta, lighting the night and heralding a rain of sand and stone. The explosion was followed by a second, and then a third.

"Jesus!" Angie said. "What the hell was that?"

"It must have been Cleomente," Doctor Sambucci said, his tone lost somewhere between awe and terror. "His powers truly are great."

Angie had no time for Sambucci's gawking or worrying about a trap. If they were going to get the Codex, they had to do it now. She snapped to her feet, heaved Sambucci to his, and they sprinted for the church.

"Were those your friends out there?" Doctor Sambucci said.

"Not my friends," Angie replied. "And dead now, more than likely."

Angie kicked open the church's front door, pushed Doctor Sambucci inside, and then slammed them shut. She found a chair nearby and wedged the door shut. It wasn't much, but it was better than nothing.

Doctor Sambucci ran down the center aisle to the altar. The church was relatively bare, with little ornamenting it besides stained glass windows and a large unpainted sandstone statue depicting the Crucifixion of Christ mounted behind the pulpit.

"Any idea where they put it?" Angie said, taking a moment to recheck the bullets in her Colt Paterson. "I can't imagine they'd just leave it…"

"Aha!"

On the altar, resting beside an ordinary Bible, was the Codex. Sambucci gently ran his hand over the book's cover before holding it up for Angie to see.

"Here it is, safe and sound," he said. Angie couldn't help but shake her head and groan.

"What is with these miracle workers leaving this thing just laying around unguarded?" she said, joining Doctor Sambucci by the altar. She noticed the only other apparent exit was a small side door just to the right of the pulpit, which she dearly hoped exited out into the desert.

"Ignorance, Mrs. Grissom," Doctor Sambucci said, flipping through the weathered ancient pages. "They do not appreciate just how important this book is."

At that, the doors behind them smashed open and inches-long splinters scattered across the room. Brother Cleomente, followed by five armed men, strutted in amidst a cloud of smoke and dust. He threw a charred thing, which by the shape of it Angie believed must have been Abbot Moore, into the center aisle ahead of him. It landed with a sickening splat. The church quickly filled with a stench like burnt pork.

"I assure you, Doctor," Brother Cleomente hissed. "I appreciate the power of that book more than you ever will."

Angie stepped in front of Doctor Sambucci and, ignoring all the others, aimed her Colt Paterson at Brother Cleomente. Cleomente's men leveled their rifles in her direction and fanned out to either side, hoping to surround her. Brother Cleomente remained motionless and unperturbed, like some saintly statue.

"I can also appreciate your dogged determination, bounty hunter, but it is finally over," Brother Cleomente said. "You are alone now. It is over."

Angie pulled back the hammer on her pistol.

"No it ain't," she said.

Brother Cleomente grimaced.

"Put that away."

"I think I'd prefer to hold on to it," Angie said. Doctor Sambucci clenched onto her duster with both fists. She could feel him trembling.

"I hope you have a plan..." Doctor Sambucci said. Angie hazarded a glance over her shoulder and saw he was ashen too. Cleomente nodded and his men began to close in.

"I had no quarrel with you, bounty hunter, but you just could not let this go," Brother Cleomente said. "Since you will only continue to serve as an obstacle, you leave the Brotherhood no choice. No choice at all."

Angie held firm. Her bullets may be of no use against Brother Cleomente, but she might be fast enough to shoot at least one or two of Cleomente's men before they tore her to pieces. That might be enough time for Doctor Sambucci to make a run for it, and with any luck at least he would make it out alive. Perhaps…

A loud howl pierced the silence.

One of Cleomente's men lowered his rifle.

"What was that?"

A blur of fur and fangs burst through a stained glass window and pounced on the poor henchman, a geyser of blood spraying a globbed cloud of scarlet stifling his screams as his head was torn off with a single violent tug. Andrew Carnation, his transformation from Man to Man-Coyote complete, stood drenched in scarlet and glanced hungrily at the gawking men around him with scarlet eyes. Even Brother Cleomente was taken aback: clearly he hadn't predicted this intrusion.

Angie did.

Chapter Nine

Taking advantage of Andrew's grisly entrance, Angie took a shot at Cleomente. He shouted, clutched his right shoulder, and fell.

Angie pushed Doctor Sambucci and dove behind the altar as the church erupted into a firefight. The remaining four Brotherhood gunmen fired not on her, though, but on Andrew the Man-Coyote. Regular bullets were little more than an irritation for him, though, producing mere flesh wounds and bruises. When they could hit him, that is. The Man-Coyote lashed out at the two men nearest to him, and slashed through them with ease. Angie poked her head out from behind the altar for a moment, but one good look at Andrew's face confirmed her worst fear: there was nothing human in those eyes, just the murderous bloodlust of a satanic beast.

"What in all that is holy is that?!" Doctor Sambucci said, covering his ears in a vain effort to block out the cacophony of gunfire, howls, and frantic screams.

"A Man-Coyote," Angie said.

"A what?" He looked as if he were trying to piece together a riddle (at least, when he didn't seem about to piss his pants). He was a smart man, perhaps he would be able to deduce the beast's identity without her ever having to spell it out. "You mean a werewolf? What is it doing here of all places?"

Brother Cleomente, bloodied but nonplussed after being shot, tore off his monk's robes to reveal a bronze barreled chest and muscles rippled with strength. With a great howl of his own he launched himself at Andrew and slugged the Man-Coyote in the snout with enough force to send even it stumbling.

THAT got his attention.

Andrew roared and kicked Cleomente in the chest. The miracle worker flew back at least a half dozen yards, smashed through one pew and landed in another. Andrew was upon Brother Cleomente again in an instant. The Man-Coyote held him down with those enormous clawed hands, opened its maw and attempted to bite off the miracle worker's head. At the last moment Brother Cleomente clutched Andrew's jaws, held them open and the creature back (but just barely). The two grappled this way for at least a minute, Cleomente's admirable fortitude against the unstoppable unbridled strength at the Man-Coyote's disposal. Then, Cleomente drove his knee into

Andrew's gut and broke himself free. Brother Cleomente had only just regained his footing when the Man-Coyote roared and charged again, this time slamming Cleomente into and - to Angie's amazement - through a wall. The two tumbled into the mission's courtyard.

"We have to run," Angie said. "Now!"

Angie and Doctor Sambucci bolted toward the side door, opposite the direction Andrew and Cleomente were brawling. She slammed into it shoulder first and smashed it open, her momentum launching her past and into the wall only a couple of feet beyond. Doctor Sambucci, always close behind, barely avoided being shot in the back as bullets struck the door frame as he dove past. Angie leaned back out the door and fired her Colt Paterson blindly at Cleomente's remaining goons before turning after Sambucci, who was already running ahead down the narrow hallway. The groan and clatter she heard behind her confirmed she'd hit something.

They ran to the end of the hall and out another door, which led to a stairwell. Doctor Sambucci hesitated, but Angie pushed him forward - no time to think about it when men were chasing you. The stairs led to the top of the mission's outer wall, granting a grand view of the inferno engulfing the desert outside and the fisticuffs in the courtyard. Brother Cleomente, bloodier but otherwise not seeming any weaker than before, used the freedom the outdoors provided to hurl Andrew across the whole length of the courtyard. Angie and Doctor Sambucci couldn't help but skid to a halt and stare, aghast, that this demonstration of the miracle worker's immense physical strength. The

Man-Coyote landed on his feet, snarled, and then charged at the miracle worker again. Brother Cleomente placed a hand on the ground at his feet. A moment later, the earth under the Man-Coyote erupted into pillars of stone, smacking him with enough brute force to kill an ordinary man and carrying Andrew higher than the church's bell tower. Then the pillars vanished, dissolved back into a shower of dust as if what had appeared to be stone was mere soil forced together so tightly by miraculous forces so as to take on the strength and appearance of granite. Andrew fell forty feet with a surprised yelp and landed snout-first beside the sinkhole where the pillar had once stood.

Angie didn't have time to watch any more, though, before she and Sambucci were set upon - not by the gunman, as she expected, but the last surviving Harpy. It swooped down from straight above and knocked Angie over the side of the wall, and only gut instinct drove her to move fast enough to reach out and grab the ledge.

"Mrs. Grissom!" Doctor Sambucci said.

The Harpy swooped out over the desert, through the smoke cloud billowing from the crater were the Order had made their stand, and then came back for another pass. It stretched its talons and did its best to pluck Doctor Sambucci from the wall. He ducked behind a battlement and the creature soared past in a blur of feathers. It screeched in annoyance.

Only now did the last Brotherhood gunman reach the roof, and found Doctor Sambucci alone and unarmed. He grinned, slung the rifle over his shoulder, and drew a rusted bowie knife from his belt.

"You've sullied the house of God with the blood of his servants," he said. "It's about time you suffered the Lord's justice…"

Angie pulled herself up just as the Brotherhood goon walked by and grabbed him from behind in a headlock. His arms failed as he choked, but his desperate strength was enough to pull Angie back atop the wall. Angie kicked him away, then reached for her pistol -

"Oh shit." She felt only air. Her Colt Paterson was gone! "Where is it?"

The Brotherhood goon bounced back, lunging at her with the knife. Angie grabbed his wrist, side stepped, and used his own momentum to slam her shoulder into his face. Two hard knocks for one day were apparently too much for it, though: she heard a pop and felt a surge of pain. Angie shrieked a curse, but did not stop.

The two struggled. Angie slammed the goon's hand against the battlement again and again until the knife at last slipped from his fingers, spinning off into the courtyard below. Pushing a boot against an outer battlement, she slammed the goon backward into the inner battlement behind them. Angie turned and delivered a left hook, then another.

The goon slumped to the floor, knocked cold. At least for the moment.

"Help!" Doctor Sambucci cried. "Help me!"

"Doc!"

The Harpy was atop Doctor Sambucci now. Exhausted and scoured, he could do little more than flail impotently as it gripped its talons around his arms and lifted him into the air. Angie kicked the unconscious goon aside and tore the rifle still slung over his shoulder from him. By the time she hefted it and pulled the trigger, the Harpy and Sambucci were over the battlefield Cleomente and Carnation had transformed the courtyard into. The Harpy screeched and both fell, landing in a heap and loud thump.

"Anne!" Brother Cleomente, who had managed to lock an arm around the Man-Coyote's neck and was trying (albeit in vain) to strangle his opponent, tossed Andrew aside in a burst of rage-induced strength and ran to the Harpy's side. It was alive, but by its movements it was wounded and its left wing appeared broken. Doctor Sambucci was motionless. Cleomente looked up and locked eyes with Angie.

She could, quite literally, feel his fury.

"Well, that ain't good."

Angie tossed the rifle, ran, and dove moments before the world became very loud and very bright. A cataclysmic explosion rocked the mission, powerful enough to fling Angie another few yards further and deafen her temporarily. When her senses returned and she looked back, she saw the section of wall she'd been atop (and the unconscious goon she'd left behind) had been vaporized, leaving behind just rubble.

Angie pulled herself back onto her feet again, and cringed at the pains that shot up her legs. Something in her leg was certainly pulled, and the way her side hurt suggested at least one cracked rib. Below, Andrew had begun a new assault on Brother Cleomente and the two had resumed their wrestling match. Closer by, she spotted Doctor Sambucci still laying where he'd fallen but the Harpy nowhere in sight.

As carefully and quickly as she could manage, Angie climbed down the ruined wall. At the bottom, a glint of metal caught her eye amidst the rubble and debris.

"Why, hello there," Angie said, plucking her Colt Paterson from between a couple scraps of ruined stone. "For a few minutes there, I thought I'd lost you."

She kissed it.

"Should've known better than that," she said.

She knelt beside the wall, fished some extra cartridges from her belt, and reloaded before making her way to Doctor Sambucci, keeping her profile low in an effort to avoid Cleomente's attention. He was knocked cold, but from the way his chest rose and fell Angie knew he was still alive.

She shook Doctor Sambucci. He stirred and opened his eyes.

"Good," she said. "Can't have you be dead now, Doc."

"I…" Doctor Sambucci said.

Then, his eyes widened.

Angie spun, drew the Colt Paterson, and unloaded all five rounds. The last Harpy, standing little more than an arm's length away, gurgled a response and toppled, five crimson holes poked into its breast.

Angie exhaled.

Chapter Ten

"Do not move, or I will kill him."

Brother Cleomente knelt over Andrew, his knee pressed against the back of the Man-Coyote's neck and a hand crackling with electricity rested atop the beast's growling head. The creature snarled and struggled but lay splayed out on its stomach, its limbs frozen as if chained in place by invisible irons. Cleomente himself glared through clenched teeth, as if it took almost all his willpower to restrain his fury. Tears streamed down his cheeks.

"This has gone on long enough," he said. He turned his eyes on the slain Harpy for a moment. "Enough have died tonight."

Angie holstered her Colt Paterson. Doctor Sambucci, not quite himself yet, wobbled as he stood.

"This is the young man who accompanied you in Rio del Cobardes, yes?" Brother Cleomente said. Angie turned to Doctor Sambucci, but he did not seem surprised. She didn't answer. "I do not want to kill you or your friend, bounty hunter."

"You have an awfully funny way of showing that," Angie said, pointing a thumb at the crater where the Mission's east wall used to be. "That there sort of suggests the opposite."

"I apologize," Brother Cleomente said. The words were forced, as if the very syllables disgusted him. "My emotions got the better of me."

Angie raised an eyebrow.

"Let's end this and part our ways in peace," he continued. "A simple trade. If the good doctor or yourself gives me the Codex, freely, then I shall spare Mr. Carnation's life and ask the Lord to let him sleep until the sun rises and he's again freed of his...condition. If not, then...I leave his fate, and yours, in the Almighty's hands."

"You...you...!" Doctor Sambucci ran between them, sputtering. "Depraved miscreant! Where is your sense of honor?"

Brother Cleomente's smiled just a tiny bit.

"Honor?" he said. "Doctor, a greater mercy would be to end this boy's wretched life and free him from the curse that transforms him into an agent of hell every full moon. Where is the honor in letting this poor soul suffer as he has? I have the grace to do what must be done, but resist doing one good in order to achieve a greater one."

Sambucci couldn't spit out any comprehensible retort.

It took only a moment for Angie see which way the dice had to fall.

"Doc…" Angie drew her Colt Paterson again. "Give me the book."

Doctor Sambucci's face scrunched into indignant fury.

"You cannot be serious," he said. "He's blackmailing us!"

"And doing a mighty fine job of it," Angie said. She pulled back the pistol's firing hammer. "Don't make me ask again."

"This book is important!" Doctor Sambucci said. "This book holds the secrets of God, of the Universe, of life and death. Brother Cleomente says it is too powerful and dangerous, and he's right: who knows what sort of chaos fanatics like the Brotherhood could do with it! You cannot give this to them. I will not allow it."

"Doc, unless the next words out of your mouth are 'I can beat him', I'm taking that goddamn book and giving it to the goddamn miracle worker," Angie said. "I don't give a single damn about your research or what the Brotherhood means to do. I've been given a chance to save Mr. Carnation's life, and I'm taking it."

Doctor Sambucci frowned, but held up his hands. He did not move to resist as Angie pulled the Codex from his coat pocket.

"Apologies, Doc," Angie said. "But we ain't escaping like at the Penterson."

She winked. Doctor Sambucci squinted. Did he get the hint?

Angie stepped away from the professor and held up the Codex for Brother Cleomente to see.

"Give it to me," he said.

"As you say, Padre," Angie said and stepped toward him.

Then, the ground behind her exploded in a puff of dust and a scent of sulfur. Angie knocked off balance by the blast just grinned and tossed the Codex as high into the air as she could.

Brother Cleomente leapt to his feet, his eyes on the Codex as it soared upward. He was too distracted to notice Doctor Sambucci conjure up a pair of grapefruit-sized balls of flame and lob them at the Cleomente's feet. Both landed short, blasting plumes of dust and sand in the miracle worker's face. The explosions were enough to knock Brother Cleomente onto his back, stunned.

Andrew, free from Cleomente's invisible shackles, rolled and slashed at Cleomente: his claws tore deep gashes across the miracle worker's torso and right thigh. The Man -Coyote sprung at Cleomente aiming to sink his fangs into the man's throat, but despite being wounded and half-blind the miracle worker was still faster than the beast. In a single motion Cleomente righted himself, delivered a fist to Andrew's snout, and then with an invisible force pushed the Man-Coyote away. Andrew howled as he flew backwards across the courtyard, slammed into the wall encircling it, and vanished in an avalanche of sandstone and mortar.

Brother Cleomente turned his attention back to Angie and Doctor Sambucci.

A flick of the wrist, and the pair were flung through the air like puppets by piano wire. Doctor Sambucci slammed into the mission's fortified wall with a loud cracking sound, then fell and slumped over. Angie struck the ground with her wounded shoulder and nearly passed out from the pain before she slid to a halt. She coughed out dirt and saliva flecked with blood. Brother Cleomente stood, his teeth bared in a vicious grimace.

"I offered you an escape," he growled, advancing toward her. "I have given you every opportunity. Yet each time you have denied me."

With whatever strength and speed she could muster, Angie threw the empty Colt Paterson at Cleomente. It clattered just shy of the miracle worker's feet.

"This," Brother Cleomente hissed, standing over her. "This is your own doing, gunslinger."

Little bolts of electricity arced between his fingers. He looked at her, eyes seething with hatred and righteous rage. Dammit, what now? Angie rolled onto her back and felt a familiar lump press into the small of her back. He took a breath and wiped dirt from her face.

"I want to confess my sins."

Brother Cleomente's grimace gained an element of impatience in its features.

"I neither have the time nor the inclination to listen to what I imagine to be a lengthy list of trespasses," he said.

"Fine, I'll keep it short," Angie said. Brother Cleomente kneeled, his electrified hand held just an inch or so from Angie's scalp.

"I've killed three miracle workers," Angie said. Her hand, slowly, inched toward her lower back. "The first was no-good bastard by the name of McCreedy. He'd been a Mainliner once, but he'd fallen off the path on account of his drinking and whoring. Gotten himself into banditry, even got himself his own gang. Then, he murdered my husband, Elijah. The second, he was a crazed madman from the Order, a compatriot of the miracle workers you broiled out there in the desert. Mr. Carnation and I tracked him to a farmhouse in Utah, where Mr. Carnation maimed him and I shot him dead. In the back."

"And the third?"

Angie smiled sweetly. Her hand clasped the grip holstered under her backside.

"Why, dear Thaddeus, that would be you."

Angie rolled, then pulled the .38's trigger.

The revolver barked.

Brother Cleomente screamed, his hands clamped over where the bullet had entered his cheek. Blood spewed from where it left the top of his skull.

Angie drew the revolver, swung, and bashed its handle into the side of Cleomente's head: he crumpled and fell. She crawled atop him and punched him once more, just to be sure.

He passed out.

Angie didn't bother to check if Cleomente was still alive, she only had two things on her mind now: Doctor Sambucci and Andrew. Well, three if she counted the incredible bonfire of pain and fatigue that coursed throughout her body. She forced herself to stand and swayed a moment as she overcame a dire urge to pass out herself.

"Mrs. Grissom!"

Angie turned: Doctor Sambucci, clutching the Codex

at his side, limped toward her.

Angie spat. The air was now quite thick with smoke and the stench of the dead.

"We need to-"

Part of the wall collapsed, debris tumbled, and Andrew the Man-Coyote stood. He noticed the Moon and howled. The beast that had once been Andrew turned, its scarlet eyes focused on Angie like twin glowing reticules. Angie raised her revolver. The creature bared its teeth, bits of flesh and blood stained and stuck in between.

"Back down, Mr. Carnation."

A long time ago, though perhaps not as long as she'd convinced herself, Angie had developed the habit of counting after threatening to shoot Andrew.

One...two...

It growled and took a step forward, the command fell on deaf inhuman ears.

...seven...eight...

She was stalling, she knew it. She watched at the Man-Coyote prowled ever closer, its eyes never moving from her, its muscles primed to pounced.

...eleven...twelve...

Doctor Sambucci took several steps back.

"Christ in Heaven," he said. What are you waiting for...?!"

"Shut it, Doc."

"That is NOT your friend, Mrs. Grissom." Doctor Sambucci sounded more stern than terrified, despite his words. "It's a monster! Shoot it before it slaughters us both!"

"I said SHUT IT."

He was right, though. There was no question about whether or not to shoot. One shot...that's all...and his pain would be over. One shot, just like the hundreds of others she'd fired over the last seven years.

One...

Only one...

Oh God, she could only picture those eyes as Andrew's eyes!

The Man-Coyote pounced. Angie fired.

Chapter Eleven

"Andrew!"

Angie sprinted to where the Man-Coyote had fallen. He was alive, but whimpering in pain and matted with blood. She kneeled beside him.

"Andrew, look at me!" she said. "Do you understand me?"

He looked at her and this time she could see the soul behind those red irises again. The Man-Coyote shuddered and sputtered blood - the bullet had struck him in the right lung. Angie tore off her sleeve, wadded the cloth, and pressed it against the wound. It soaked in a matter of seconds.

"God dammit…Doc! Doc, where are you?"

This wasn't happening. Not here. Not like this!

"I am right here, Mrs. Grissom," Doctor Sambucci

said, though he stood about a yard away.

"He's bleeding out!"

Even in the dark, Angie could tell that he was queasy.

"Yes, I can see that," he said.

"Well?"

The Doctor did not answer.

"Do something!" If Angie weren't busy trying to hold back the blood, she'd have shoved her gun into Sambucci's gut. "Heal him!"

"With what?" he said. "I told you, I'm not a miracle worker!"

"You're a doctor!"

Sambucci huffed, indignant.

"Not that sort of doctor, madam."

Enough of this! Angie grabbed her .38 and, with one hand still pressed on Andrew's bullet wound, aimed the revolver at the Doctor.

"He dies, and I swear to God I will not hesitate to blow your brains all over this place and leave your stinkin' corpse for the buzzards!" Angie roared. "Do something!"

Sambucci seemed nonplussed by the threat.

"How long has Mr. Carnation suffered from Physical Lycanthropy?" he said.

"From what?"

"How long has he been a werewolf?" Doctor Sambucci said. "And when did you ever plan to inform me of his condition? Or, were you intending to never reveal that minor detail?"

Angie let her arm fall to her side and focused again on the wound.

"We call 'em Man-Coyotes out here," she said. "He caught it years ago down in Texas. Picked him up not long after and been keeping him tamed ever since."

Doctor Sambucci raised an eyebrow.

"Tamed?"

Angie hesitated. Only Uncle Joshua had any idea what Andrew really was, and he was decent enough to feign obliviousness. She'd never spoken of Andrew's condition with anyone before. No point in keeping it hidden now, though, not with Andrew bleeding out in her arms.

"I chain him up before it begins," she muttered. "Does it really matter? Please…"

Doctor Sambucci sighed.

"I…" He paused. Suddenly, his head tilted and his eyes lit up. "Wait, of course! The Codex!"

He pulled the book from his cloak, tossed it to the floor and began to leaf through it wildly. Andrew coughed up more blood, looked at Angie, and whimpered again.

"You're gonna be fine, Mr. Carnation, just stay calm," she said. She knew she was crying, but did her best to pretend she wasn't. Now wasn't the time for weakness. "The Doc will fix you up. You'll see."

Andrew reached with his left hand and began to scratch letters in the dirt with his claws.

"SORRY"

"No need for apologies," Angie said. "You and I both knew this would happen eventually, it was just the nature of the thing."

He drew again:

"LET GO"

He looked at her again, pleading. No. No, she wouldn't be having that. Not again.

"Don't you be doing that now," she said, laughing a little without meaning to. "You ain't dying here in the middle of goddamned nowhere. I ain't letting you."

Doctor Sambucci groaned.

"Blasted scribbles..." he said, though Angie was sure he didn't mean for her to hear.

"You better not be preparing to tell us that we dragged you and that good-for-nothing book halfway across the desert for it to be of no use when we actually need it, Doc."

"No...no...no..." Andrew paused on a page, his finger running down a couple of particular lines. "Hm. This seems promising. Yes...yes, if Cardinal Pelletier's hypothesis is correct, then this just might work!"

"What will?"

He ignored her.

"Wait here!"

Doctor Sambucci, after a brief stumble, ran off for what remained of the church.

"Doc! Doc, where the hell are you going?"

Andrew coughed again and whimpered. His eyes fluttered shut. Angie bopped him on the nose, startling him away again.

"No! Bad dog," she said. "I said you ain't dying here, and I meant it."

Sambucci returned with an armful of vials and things. He let them scatter on the ground as he kneeled again.

"What's all this?" Angie said.

Again, Sambucci ignored her. He returned to the

book, his finger running across several lines. He unscrewed a bottle, then poured oil on Andrew's forehead and a second dab on his chest. He flinched and snarled. Sambucci hesitated a moment, as if he only now remembered that he was within arm's reach of a Man-Coyote.

"P-please, Mr. Carnation, you must…must let me work," he stuttered. He smeared the oil, then retrieved a branch of some plant Angie didn't recognize, crushed it, and then started spreading the powder.

"I don't appreciate the mystery, Doc," Angie said.

"Mr. Carnation's condition is not well understood, nor easy to treat," Doctor Sambucci said, speaking as he continued applying powders and oils. "There are two schools of thought in regards to physical Lycanthropy: that it is either a curse or a disease. In 1749, the esteemed Cardinal Pelletier of Tours conducted a study of lycanthropy and wrote an extensive early treatise on the subject. He took the position that lycanthropy was a particularly virulent curse and suggested that a powerful enough Saint could lift it."

"We seem to be short one Saint, Doc," Angie said. "Unless you're proposing we try rousing Brother Cleomente over there, which I think would not be our best interests…"

"Ah, but we have the Codex!" Doctor Sambucci said. "We don't need a Saint, just the method needed to properly purify the soul."

"That's nice, but what the hell does all of that have to do with his damned bullet wound?"

Doctor Sambucci bit his lip.

"I couldn't find the page explaining how to heal a wound this serious," he said. "But I did manage to find the page detailing purification. If Cardinal Pelletier is right, then purification may lift his curse, or at the very least heal the wound."

Sambucci places one hand on Andrew's forehead and another on his chest.

"You may wish to stand back."

Angie did so as he began to mutter...not Aramaic or Latin, as a Miracle Worker would, but some unfamiliar gibberish. The air grew heavier, the wind picked up, and she could swear that both man and man-beast seemed to almost shimmer - as if each were in daylight but had been transposed into this night scene. As the scene progressed, both seemed to convulse as one would being electrocuted. As the convulsions grew more severe, Angie tried to step toward them but felt as if some invisible force was pushing her away.

"Andrew! Doc!"

A clap of thunder drowned out her words and a moment later, it was done. Sambucci collapsed, still seizing, but his convulsions weakening. The Man-Coyote was still. Fearing the worst Angie rushed back to his side, but as she neared she saw that despite the blood she could no longer see the wound in his chest. What seemed to be stillness was in fact the calm shallow breaths of one asleep. Whatever Doctor Sambucci had done, it hadn't freed Andrew of his curse but at least it seemed to have saved his life.

Chapter Twelve

"My lung hurts."

Angie rolled her eyes as she finished tying off her horse to the hitching post. With the miracle workers from the Order little more than cinders in the desert, it seemed only reasonable they kept the mares they'd ridden out on.

"Ugh, this again?" Angie said. "Really, Mr. Carnation, this is hardly the first time you've met the business end of a pistol."

"Well…yes, that's true…"

He carefully lowered himself from his own steed, swatting away Angie's hand as she reached to help. He grunted as his boots landed a bit harder than he'd hoped: after the one-monster war he fought with Brother Cleomente, it was clear to Angie he'd be hurting for days at least. The boy had a tendency to heal up quick from even the worst wounds, though. A booby prize for having to suffer the horror of the transformations, she supposed.

"…But, that ain't the point!"

Doctor Sambucci, his mare having been the first hitched, slapped Andrew on the back. It was light, but still enough for the Cajun's eyes to near pop out of his head from the blow.

"I'm sure Mrs. Grissom does not intend to make shooting her business associates a regular occurrence," he said. By his tone of voice and his casual smile, Angie might've mistaken the gesture as the simple friendly advice it seemed. After riding with these two for the last few days, however, it was clear the good Doctor was enjoying prodding Andrew as much as Andrew enjoyed prodding him prior to his kidnapping.

"Besides, the mitigating circumstances…"

Andrew just glared.

"Embrasse moi tchew, Doc," he muttered.

After Andrew's return, the ride from El Abeto Violeta had been unremarkable. Tedious even, between Andrew's complaints and Doctor Sambucci's pedantic ramblings. Good lord, it was like being a little girl trapped in that schoolhouse all over again! Angie had never been more relieved to see the dingy rooftops of Verdopolis again.

Not wasting any time, they rode directly to the courthouse. The Verdopolis Courthouse was probably the fanciest thing in town, and at three stories was about the tallest too. The outside was lined with muddy red brick, sanded down smooth, with the occasional window lined with pale pine frames. The front boasted a large and wide granite staircase which, along with the four white columns and the squat copper dome, gave the impression of a poor man's Capitol Building. It was surrounded by a wall of rounded decorative shrubs that were more yellow than green.

As they reached those steps, Doctor Sambucci paused.

"You ain't gettin' cold feet, are you?" Andrew said. "I'd hate to have to shoot you now, after all that ruckus."

Sambucci just smiled and gently shook his head. Before he could reply, another voice interrupted:

"Oh! Mrs. Grissom! Hello!"

Wilson, a dumb grin plastered between those bulging cheeks, plodded down the courthouse steps toward them. The sight reminded Angie of a Saint Bernard greeting its master at the door.

"G'morning, Wilson."

Wilson took a moment to catch his breath, he was unused to exercise more strenuous than lifting a fountain pen.

"I have been trying to get in touch with you for days," he said. "Did your uncle pass along my message?"

Angie raised an eyebrow.

"Message?"

At first Wilson grimaced at her answer, but upon noticing Doctor Sambucci his eyes grew a bit rounder and his complexion a bit more waxen. He held a hand to his lips, as if to hold back a terrified gasp.

"Oh dear," he said.

That couldn't be a sign for anything good.

"Wilson..." Angie said, but his eyes were fixated on the Easterner.

"I take it that this fellow is Mr. Sambucci?" Wilson squeaked.

"Doctor." Sambucci straightened his eyeglasses. "Doctor Celeron Sambucci, of Harvard."

Wilson turned from waxen to ashen at that.

"Oh dear."

Andrew grumbled. After everything, he wasn't amused by this performance.

"You got something to say?" Andrew said. The Cajun was never fond of the diplomatic touch Angie usually used with their bondsman, thus why she didn't often bring him around to Wilson's office.

"Oh. Well, you see, I..." Wilson said, stammering. He cut himself off and turned back to Angie. "Are you certain you did not get my message? I was rather adamant it be delivered posthaste..."

Enough of this!

"Wilson!"

Wilson froze, as if worried what a false move on his part would end with. He took a breath, scrunched his eyes shut, and blurted:

"There is no bounty."

Andrew shouted a series of obscenities at the burly bondsman, although the only word Angie understood was the only one on her own mind:

"WHAT?!"

Wilson backed away and held up his hands, a terrified grin even larger than the dumb one he initially sported sneaking onto his lips.

"I-I swear to you, I did not know when I offered it!" he said.

Andrew quaked with fury. Doctor Sambucci just appeared confused. Angie's hand had, of its own volition, maneuvered itself to her Colt Paterson's hilt.

"I do not understand," Doctor Sambucci said.

"It was a simple misunderstanding, sir, I assure you-"

"God damn coullion!" Andrew was maybe thirty seconds from strangling the buffoon. "I was just about killed for this job! Twice!"

"I'm sorry for the inconvenience," Wilson said. "But..."

The bail bondsman was interrupted by Angie's fist colliding with his face.

Pain erupted, an electric burst of discomfort that zapped from her knuckles to her wrist in a split instant. This was good hurting though, hurting that served a very specific and quite righteous purpose. Beyond her fist she heard the familiar crackle, a sound that combined with the pain she - for just a moment - worried may have come from herself. Wilson, his fat cheeks wobbling and eyes squeezed tighter than the belt around his waist, recoiled.

He opened those eyes, blinked, and then collapsed in a blobby unconscious heap. Blood trickled from his (probably) broken nose.

"Mrs. Grissom!" Doctor Sambucci said. "That was uncalled for!"

Angie shook the pain from her hand, ignoring the gawks from bystanders they were now attracting.

"No, Doc," she said. "That was a long, long time coming. Besides, it ain't the first time I've disciplined him."

From amidst the onlookers emerged one man who laughed and applauded at the show. As the fellow clapped and walked down the steps toward them, Angie recognized him. She removed her bowler.

"Howdy, Judge."

"Ah, Mrs. Grissom! What an unexpected pleasure. Stunning as always!" Judge Breckenridge said, stepping over the moaning half-conscious form of his dear friend so he could kiss Angie's cheek. He nodded toward Andrew, but upon seeing Sambucci he paused, smiled, and offered his hand.

"I don't believe you and I have been acquainted. Doctor Sambucci, isn't it? Elmer Breckenridge."

Elmer Breckenridge was not, at first glance, an imposing man. If anything, Angie thought he most resembled a kindly old salesman, the sort of man who'd give away free candies to little children at his corner shop. He had a smile that disarmed you with its sincerity. Breckenridge stood a bit on the short side, and his short curly hair went entirely white long ago. Behind those little round glasses, though, were eyes that betrayed his true nature as a man of frightening intelligence and ambition. That he had maintained such an intimate friendship with a cowardly weasel like Wilson was a fact that had baffled Angie since the first time they'd met.

As Breckenridge shook hands with Sambucci, Wilson moaned again.

"Oh…I think my nose is broken…" he said. Breckenridge rolled his eyes.

"Don't be so dramatic," Breckenridge muttered, then

turned to Angie: "I take it Wilson filled you in on the error?"

"I'm mildly perturbed by the news, that's for sure," Angie said, putting on her bowler again.

"Indeed."

Breckenridge motioned toward the courthouse and led the group inside. The courthouse's main lobby was small considering the apparent size of the building outside, with little room for much else beyond the large bifurcated staircase leading up to the second floor and the courtrooms within. The floors were varnished wood, but the walls were white plaster to match the colonnade out front.

"Yes, a rather unfortunate case," Breckenridge said, hands clasped together behind his back. "A result of miscommunication on behalf of our dear friends, the Knights of Saint James, I'm afraid."

"Who?" Andrew said. Angie sighed and shook her head.

"The monks who have guarded the Codex since the times of Christ," Doctor Sambucci said. "What sort of miscommunication?"

"My understanding, Doctor, is that the gentleman who granted you permission to take the rather ancient tome under your arm did not inform his brothers," Breckenridge said, leading them through a side door and down a hall. "A mere slip of the mind, it seems. When it was discovered that the Codex was missing and that you had left, the worst was presumed and a Monk was dispatched to report a theft."

Andrew groaned.

"And by the time they figured the mistake, it'd been too late?"

"Exactly."

Breckenridge stopped before a large double door, a bronze plaque with his name bolted into one. He fished out a key, unlocked it, and opened to reveal a lavish office: plush green carpeting, a fifteen-foot tall ceiling, a large mahogany desk littered with neatly stacked piles of paperwork, two large bookshelves taking up the walls to both Angie's left and right. The first time Angie had seen this office, she had been impressed. Not now, though.

"So, there is no reward," Angie said, though the answer was obvious.

"Rescinded, I'm sorry to say," Breckenridge said. "Forgive me, Mrs. Grissom, but there really is nothing I can do except to offer the deepest appreciation of the United States government for tracking down the good doctor and delivering him to us."

Defeated, Angie chose the nearest leather chair and let herself collapse into it. After all the trouble it took to get Sambucci - and trouble was the polite way to describe it - there was nothing? Maybe Uncle Joshua was right: she was in the wrong business after all.

Breckenridge opened a lower drawer in his desk and retrieved an olive-colored bottle of what only could be liquor, as well as several small shot glasses.

"Care for a drink?" he said.

"No, thank you," Doctor Sambucci said. Angie just shook her head. Andrew shrugged.

"I think I could do for a spot of whiskey," he said. Breckenridge smiled wide, then poured.

"Ah! There's my man!" Breckenridge said. "Two

whiskeys it is."

They drank, Andrew finishing his whiskey in a single gulp.

"Now," Breckenridge said. "Tell me, what happened in Rio del Cobardes?"

+ + +

Angie excused herself from Breckenridge's office and left, unwilling to hear the whole fiasco be recounted. Andrew, at least, barely noticed - he got that way when he was excited and in the midst of tale-telling. Fiasco, that was certainly the word. What in God's good name was the point of all this hardship? It wasn't the first time Angie had failed to get paid for a job, but never before had Wilson sent her off to chase a bounty the Law didn't even want. Two jobs, now. Two tough jobs in a row she's bled on and no pay. As she walked down the courtyard steps, she gave her Colt Paterson a tender pat.

"What now?"

She paused at the foot of the steps and, for a moment, just watched Verdopolis: pigeons perched on the shoe store across the street, a cart hauling canisters of milk, a rabble of small children playing jacks on the corner. Why, again, was she still doing this?

"Maybe Uncle Joshua is right," she said to no one. Maybe it was time to stop after all.

"Mrs. Grissom!"

The thought broken, Angie turned and watched Doctor Sambucci following her out the courthouse.

"Oh, good! I was afraid you had gone," he said, adjusting his glasses. Then, he offered his hand. "I haven't had the opportunity to thank you. Properly, that is."

"Thank me?" Angie said. "For what?"

"For saving me, of course."

Doctor Sambucci smiled. He really had a kind, warm smile, didn't he? She took his hand.

"Just doing our jobs, Doc."

"That may be so, but I appreciate it nonetheless," Doctor Sambucci said. "If not for you, Brother Cleomente would have certainly attacked me in Rio del Cobardes and I would've been unable to stop him from taking the Codex. If not for you, who knows what the Brotherhood would have done to me. I am in your debt."

He reached into his pocket.

"Oh no, Doc, I can't…"

"Please, Mrs. Grissom, I insist," Doctor Sambucci said. He scribbled some numbers, signed, and then handed her the check. Angie's heart jumped.

"Doc…" she said. "This is more than double what Wilson was paying us!"

"Surely, Mrs. Grissom, you and Mr. Carnation deserve more than that after everything," Doctor Sambucci said. "I apologize, I wish I could reward you with more. However, I need to save my remaining funds for the trip back East."

He offered his hand again. Angie shook it wholeheartedly.

"Now if you would excuse me, I must wire my colleagues in Boston and let them know I am well," Doctor Sambucci said. Again, he smiled. "Good day."

Angie watched Doctor Sambucci until he vanished amidst the pedestrians down the road. She looked down at the check, grinned, then folded it and slipped it into her duster's inside pocket.

What had she been thinking about again?

Bah, who cared?

Time to rest up, then on to the next bounty!

About the Author

A writer for as far back as he could remember, Paul V. Cwiakala was raised on a steady diet of Science Fiction, Fantasy, and Adventure movies ranging from novels by Harry Turtledove and H. G. Wells to movies written by Shinichi Sekizawa and Lawrence Kasdan. Having written short stories throughout his youth, Paul wrote his first novel while pursuing undergraduate studies at William Paterson University, where he earned a Bachelor's Degree in Communications in 2009.

Paul published his first novel, *Fallen Saints*, through Silk Baron Independent Press in 2014. His second book, *A Slave of the Bird Men*, was published in 2016.

Also Available From
Silk Baron Independent Press

A SLAVE OF THE
BIRD MEN

A SAILOR LEFT FOR DEAD
IN A LAND WHERE BIRDS RULE!

Francisco del Puerto had dreams of gold and adventure when he joined an expedition to explore the far-off Americas. But, after a fateful encounter on the shores of the Rio De La Plata he's been left stranded and at the mercy of the Bird Men—a race of intelligent birds inhabiting a South America very different from the one history knew. Taken as a slave by the enigmatic Lord Ereter, can Francisco learn to live and survive among them in this strange new world?

Adventure and Survival in a South America that never was!

www.ingramcontent.com/pod-product-compliance
Lightning Source LLC
Chambersburg PA
CBHW030231180626
46810CB00008B/3070